Madness and

Over the past 5 years, there have been so many twists and turns on the path that I have walked, that to write my story would fill more pages than you'd care to find in any book. I have said it before though, and I will say it again, I am no writer. There is no novel inside of me, bursting to make it onto the page, I have neither the skills, the academic background, nor the attention span to be anything other than a scribbler. I have become quite affectionate of that term too, I much prefer scribbles and scribbler, to poems or poet.
It seems that during my times of emotional upheaval, immense sadness, or overwhelming delight, that words fall out of me. Much the same that tears will fall with others, or that they might punch the air for joy, for me a line will fall into my mind. It is now compulsion to scribble that line, and when I do, the piece creates itself in front of me, and I have no real idea what it will be until the last word is formed.
Everything that you read within these pages is 100% pure emotional outlet, these are my smiles, cries, sighs, lows and highs.
The biggest surprise to me is that when these scribbles are formed, just how many and how deeply people have connected with them on my Facebook page.
It seems that so many of us are going through such similar emotional journeys, and yet we feel that we are travelling them alone. It has been amazing to witness a coming together of people, in sadness, in heartbreak and in happiness. My page has become almost a community, and the comments that flow are incredible to read. People saying they relate, that they resonate, that they feel less alone, just from connecting with a particular piece, and for a scribbler that gives me such a buzz to hear.
I have only just realised myself, after these comments, and many conversations with people who follow, that this has been my coping mechanism for the traumas that life deals me.
I feel an overwhelming sense of pride, and of achievement, that I have learned that these words, these scribbles, my thoughts and feelings, have in fact become part of the coping mechanism, and healing process of other people too.

Madness and Therapy

They're not all pretty pieces, and they're often dark to read back, and yet even these have been met with positive reactions. I guess when we're going through the shit times, we don't always need a message of motivation, we don't always need someone to say, "it'll all be better soon."
Maybe, just maybe, sometimes, all we need to be able to see and hear, is that somebody else has felt this too. That it is normal to go through it. That we are not failing to cope, and not being beaten by anything, but that we're simply going through the same rollercoaster that everyone else is too.
Maybe, knowing someone else is sitting in the darkness with you, is a greater comfort than someone telling you to find the light.
As much respect as I do have for those positive affirmations, I feel that I have discovered through my page, that more power comes from giving another a perspective that is on the same level as they currently are, rather than offering a view from a step that is so much further away, and just looks too big to take.

This book begins with a thank you for all who have helped me get this far, that's you, that's every person that has ever read me. The last piece in the book describes better, what I have been trying to say here, that it is the pain, that binds us all together.

If you are holding this book in your hands right now, then I truly hope that somewhere withing these pages, you can find even one word that helps you in some way, or that will bring a smile or two your way also.

Thank you

Mesentire

aka

R.Cuthbert

Madness and Therapy

For Fran, taken from us without warning, and no chance to say goodbye. I still blow you kisses. R.I.P x

For Billie Jo, my big sister who was stolen from us to fly with the angels. I miss you sis, wish you were here. x

For my Mother, Marie, who beat all the odds, proved all the doctors wrong and somehow, miraculously, is still with us today after suffering a heart attack while swimming and being found, drowned, and told she would never wake up. I am very happy that you're still here to be able to read this. Love you Mum. x

For my Dad, Rog, that man's a warrior the way he has just took over all roles to be cook, cleaner and bottle washer, to be 24hr carer for my mum, and always there with a beer and a cigar for me. I'm proud of you Dad. x

For every person who tried to kick me when I was down, lied, cheated and stole moments of happiness that should have been mine. Thank you for the material.

For Vicky, the love of my life, without who, I wouldn't have got through any of the above. The girl is a rock. She has lifted me, laughed with me, and let me cry upon her shoulder. Mostly, she has taught me that there really are people out there, who mean what they say. Honest, true, sincere, and cute as fuck too btw. My cool counterpart in life, and a stone cold fox. Love you Vicky. x

Madness and Therapy

Madness and Therapy

Contents

1. Scribbles
2. Rain Cloud And Doubt
3. The Future We Don't Know
4. Chapter And Verse
5. In The Darkness That You Find Yourself
6. The Narcissist
7. Little Miss Suburbia
8. A Penny For Your Thoughts
9. Chapters
10. (cont.)
11. The Questioning Within Your Heart
12. The Penthouse Of Your Problems
13. The Point Of No Return
14. More
15. Nightmare
16. The Joker
17. Flyers And Fallers
18. Be My Angel
19. The Affair
20. Stay
21. It's OK
22. Talking In Our Sleep
23. Playlists
24. Rainbows
25. If The Seeds I Plant Stop Growing
26. Power In The Pain
27. Meet The Real Me
28. My Spark
29. The Girl That Has It All
30. Don't Say A Word
31. My Sister
32. Hiatus
33. To The Wire
34. The Devils Cup
    a. Eclipse

35. Dawning Love
36. Do Not Just Be
37. Resurrect
38. Survival
39. Royal Romance
40. A Hundred Feet Tall
41. Fools Gold
42. Moon Beams
    a. Singe
43. In The Storm
44. Heads or tails
45. Pipe Dreams And Lullabies
46. (cont.)
47. Serial Spiller
48. The Art Of Letting Go
49. You've Got This
50. The Void
51. Before The Storm
52. Moon Secrets
    a. Wants In A Lifetime
53. A Little Darkness
    a. Lonely Eyes
54. The Mirror Man
55. Regrets
    a. Playing With Fire
56. Beauty In The Breakage
57. Smoke And Mirrors
58. One Chance
59. 16/05/2020
60. Amor Fati
61. Whisper To An Angel
62. It's All You
63. One Man Band
64. Pillow Talk
65. Weary Eyes
66. Fran
67. Perfection To My Passions

68. Let's Get Some Air
69. Smiles And Sighs
    a. Strong
70. Balloon Heart
71. Wear Your Crown
72. Your Wings
    a. Calming Influence
73. I Don't Mind
74. Time And Space
75. Farewell Friend
76. Old Romantics
77. Grief
78. Big Surprise
79. The Girl Who Grew Too Fast
80. Bitterness
81. One More Step
82. Miss You Days
83. Narcissist Heart
84. Smiles And Cries
85. Lost Youth
86. Caged
87. The Language Of Two Lovers
88. Kindred Spirit
89. Troubled Pasts
90. Mosaic
91. Don't Forget, No Regret
92. Red Flags
    a. Stupid Love
93. Marionette 1
94. Marionette 2
95. More Alive
96. Red Wine
97. My Everything
98. Overthinking
99. My Perfection
100. Treasures
101. Magical

102. What If?
103. The Future Yet Unseen
104. Contentment
105. Talking In Tongues
106. Not Alone
107. Learning To Be Me
108. Nobody Around
109. Among The Ashes
110. Paradoxical
111. The Thief Of Self Belief
112. Changed
113. Whole
114. Disdain
115. My Own Disease
116. Damn You
117. You Just Don't Get It
118. Bliss
119. Homeless Hymn
120. The Last Lost Boy
121. Embers To Ashes
122. Walking With The Stars
123. Far From Perfect, Far From Pitiful
124. You Just Can't Keep Me Down
125. Dark Dilema
126. No Placebo
127. The King Of Catastrophe
128. Dancing Feet
129. Grow Your Roses
130. The Angels
131. Walk Away
132. The Answers
133. Space To Grow
134. Some Days
135. Time To Heal
136. Cursed
137. Back Down The Rabbit Hole
138. Walk Of Shame

Madness and Therapy

139.	The Truth
140.	Unscribbled
141.	The Precipice
142.	Smitten
143.	Seaglass
144.	The Exception To The Rule
145.	Love Yourself More
146.	The Big Bad Wolf
147.	Who Am I?
148.	Take My Hand
149.	Nectar
150.	The Pain That Binds Us

SCRIBBLES

I speak as I find, and I find as I feel,
each word from emotion, to keep it all real.
No thoughts left filtered, nothing felt left unsaid,
simply laid down my truths to empty my head.
Every word, every line, some from love, some from rage,
fall from my heart and soul, onto the page.
There's a lifetime of scribbles, to be penned from my years
of laughter of heartbreak, of smiles and of tears.
With no motive in mind, just a place to express
and I find you here now, as you read and digest.
It's a wonder to me, to have even believed
that I'd be so accepted, and so well received.
I wish to say thank you, for every scribble you've read,
proving we've never, been alone as we've bled.
So to all who are winning, and all who still cry,
to all who are falling, and all that can fly,
I offer this book, as place that forever,
we can find solace in sentiments, that we share together

RAIN CLOUD AND DOUBT

I see that girl just standing on the side lines
she bows her head and almost looks ashamed.
Seems she's just waiting, for life to pass her by
she's, just about, had it with this game.
She's fought her whole life, just to lose again
and she'll never let another, see her cry.
Standing with her shadow for her only company
she just wonders, why she should even try.
I see the boy, whisper to her softly
and watch her eyes light up to what he's said
her lips begin to form a smile now
and for the first time in a while she lifts her head.

He said

Rain cloud and doubt, and muddy waters
holes in your shoes and blistered feet
troubled times, and steep hill climbs,
there's still, nothing in this life that you can't beat.
I will walk with you when you are tired and lonely
I will carry you when you feel that you will fall
I will stop and keep you warm in the cold dark nights
because together, we can really beat it all.

THE FUTURE WE DON'T KNOW

Longing for the memory
that's lingering in mind
to find the time to recreate
so I can hit rewind.
Thoughts take me back to days
when the sunlight in your eyes
was enough, in my solitude
to light up darkened skies.
Resisting what we're missing
heading onwards, looking back
and the distance growing slowly
as I walk the beaten track.
I know where I've come from
and I know that it is showing
that there's fear on my horizon
at not knowing where I'm going.
I chose to walk away from here
to give me chance to heal
and the scars upon my heart
prevent me now to feel.
Perhaps there's no forever
and perhaps now letting go
is the only way to hold on
to the future we don't know.
Some things just are, some things just be
but people aren't possessions
you love, you live, you take, you give
and each of these acts, are lessons.

CHAPTER AND VERSE

Oh you think you know me
because you heard the fairy tale
about my once upon a time,
but the truth does not prevail
in the story from the lips
in the voices that do speak
to depict me as a failure
and display this man as weak.
There are tongues more forked than snakes
who bear the names of so-called friends
who rejoice in bitter twisted lies
and the messages they send.
Oh you think you know me
because the story echoes through
the Chinese whispered words
passed along the vicious few.
A book is often judged
by the covers others make
to hide the content from a reader
with an image that is fake.
Open up instead each page
and give the time to every letter
to be digested as the words form
to paint true pictures that are better.
And I'll say this to you now
if it's the facts that you are seeking
then let the proof be in the open book
not in the sound of hatred speaking.
Oh you think you know me
because you've heard the very worse
but only will you learn me
if you read each chapter, every verse

Madness and Therapy

IN THE DARKNESS THAT YOU FIND YOURSELF

I know you've been to the bottom
and worn bruises I can't see.
I know you've lost sight of yourself
and spent time with misery.
I know the faith that used to carry you
has left you without hope,
because you reach your hands to no one
on the days that you can't cope.
I know the salted water falling,
from the corner of your eyes
is invisible to everyone,
and you lack the courage just to rise.
I know you feel it's time to give up
and you have no strength to breathe,
in the darkness that you find yourself,
that grips so hard you can't leave.
I've once been where you are now
and I know the feeling of this pain,
and I know you can defeat this
and that you'll be yourself again.
So take my arm as I embrace you
let me carry you my friend,
because one day you'll see this as beginning,
though it's feeling like the end.

THE NARCISSIST

You just don't seem to get it
that the words you always use,
lead to the feeling of destruction
and of the internal self-abuse.
You let me down like no other
and the mess you left behind,
is a broken pile of fragments
with missing pieces, I can't find.
I sneer at who you've made me
and the weakness that I feel,
that self-belief is disbelieving
that the good in me was real.
I listen when I'm told that
I am worth so much very more,
but listening is not hearing
unless you feel it in your core.
There are no bruises to be seen
and my bones are still intact,
the damage caused is so much deeper
in my soul that you attacked.
Devils dress in angels clothing
and bullies come in many guises,
with eyes that look of saviours
but a secret tongue that just chastises.
My ego and my self esteem
are the trophies that you stole,
and somehow watching me destroyed
made you feel that you were whole.
My reparation is beginning
and you no longer can devour,
the heart that begins to beat again
now that you have lost your power.

LITTLE MISS SUBURBIA

Summers now, keep rolling by,
this world is ever turning.
Matriarch and dutiful,
supressing inner yearning.
Holding back what's real, inside,
try to douse the fire.
A pillar of vanilla,
melting as the flames lick higher.
Oh little Miss Suburbia,
her eyes they cannot hide.
A songbird, looking outward,
from the cage she's trapped inside.
She sings a melancholy melody,
that floats across the air.
Desire, ever present,
in her captivating stare.

A metamorphosis of being,
this transition was not chosen.
Resistance, surely futile,
resulting only in implosion.
Leather, lace, and fantasy,
this songbird takes to flight.
A pioneer of her passions,
she's submitting to the night.
'Woman, mother, wife and lover,
freely trapped, in lies so true.
Content with ever wanting more,
the oxymoron that is you.

A PENNY FOR YOUR THOUGHTS

Come whisper me your secrets
I promise not to tell.
I'll give a penny for your thoughts
and you know I'll never sell.
Share with me every wish
that you made upon each star.
Tell me of your pains
and I'll heal every scar.
Share with me your stories
of every time you fell.
Show to me your heaven
and I'll save you from your hell.

CHAPTERS

One chapter had been closed,
from the pages in her heart
and time to find herself again,
as two souls, decide to part.
Decisions don't come easy,
and plans don't come, without great care
as trust and faith is broken,
and a guarded heart won't share.
But a time of healing passes,
and reparation is ongoing
when slowly all the needs and wants,
of a lonely heart start showing.
She opened up her eyes again,
while getting ready, to now face
the chance to write, a whole new chapter,
with arms ready to embrace.
Her defences slowly lowered,
doubting shadows begun to fade,
in walks a Knight in shining armour,
who is every wish, that she had made.
A man who cares and loves, an "equal",
he brings smiles, and he restores
the trust and faith, within
the girl he now adores.
And so happily ever after,
is here in all its glory,
but this once upon a time, it seems,
is just not a fairy story.
As time passes day by day,
inside the armour that had gleamed
was not the perfect Knight she'd seen,
but the big bad wolf, it seemed.
Turning smiles back in to tears,
turning hearts back into stone,

turning the love of being together,
into wishing to be alone.
The words that came were bitter,
harsh actions, mood unruly,
Prince charming didn't rescue,
instead came to bully, cruelly.
Chapter 3, it now transpires
is how the girl goes back to the start.
To begin again to find what's lost,
from inside, of her own heart.
She's strong and she's determined,
she knows she's worth much more,
and she knows that life will show her
that there's so much more in store.
This tale isn't quite the sweetest,
and it isn't what was sought,
it's not what dreams are made of,
so far away now from that thought.
But it is a story that shows power
and proves that she, has a wealth
of strength deep inside of her,
the girl who instead, rescued herself.

THE QUESTIONING WITHIN YOUR HEART

The turbulence of mind control
the earthquake of desire,
the tidal wave of self esteem
these forces never tire.
The constant inner argument
the knowing right from wrong,
the doing, what you have to do
against your passions strong.
The listening, without interest
to all around you, have to say,
the abysmal lack of self respect
that fills your every day.
The absolute necessity
of staying till the end,
the never-ending solitude
loneliness your only friend.
The emptiness that fills your mind
the innocence age stole,
the questioning, within your heart
the answer, in your soul.

THE PENTHOUSE OF YOUR PROBLEMS

You dream of disappearing
while you lie awake at night,
in the penthouse of your problems
and you think that you just might.
Nobody hears you screaming
because you keep it all inside,
the ghosts that haunt your heart
couldn't leave you if they tried.
There is a melody that's playing
a tune you've danced to in the past,
that freezes time just for a second
then that moment's, gone too fast.
You choose to stay instead of leaving
but said goodbye a million times,
by the way you look at what should love you
and ignoring all the signs.
Each day brings nothing new here
chained to the bed you made, to lie,
and it seems that all your living
is time passing till you die.

THE POINT OF NO RETURN

I talk too much and never say enough
but the look in my eyes shows,
in the silences that nights can bring
my hands tell her what she knows.
Fingertips that just explore
every fragment of her skin,
and to feel her lips against my own
in the moments we get lost in.
Her contours are my journey
and destination is the fire,
that I can light within her
by indulging in desire.
She's my fantasy and she'll realise
that my passions drive my greed,
to make her, give herself to me,
just to satisfy my need.
I will lose myself within her
and she'll lose herself with me,
until so close, we become one
in pure sensuality.
I see her breathing deeper
watch her bite her lip and say,
quietly, into my ear
a little prayer to guide my way.
Until the fire rages higher
and I watch her feel the burn,
I will leave her without choice
but to reach the point of no return.

MORE

I'm much more than just a little bit lost
I'm more than just confused
I'm more than just another toy
for you to discard once you've used
I'm more than just the light inside
I'm more than darkness that consumes
I'm much more than just the echo
that's heard in empty rooms
I'm more than all these voices
and I'm more than every act
I'm so much more than every broken piece
that used to be intact
I'm more than just a memory
I'm more than a dream to come
I'm more than those who doubt my being
I'm much more and then still some
I'm more than just believing
and I'm more than you'll agree
I'm so much more than the insignificance
of what you see in me

NIGHTMARE

I'm fighting with the future,
as my destiny,
suggests to me
my past still casts a shadow
on the path I choose to walk,
and talk is cheap.
My head is under water,
and I ought to,
just let go
of the arms
that caused such harm,
and cut me deep.
I can't breathe, while not believing,
there's no reason to be grieving
for the living,
without giving
me my worth.
I can't scream inside this dream,
and I seem
to be aware,
I live a nightmare
as I walk upon this earth.

THE JOKER

I am the joker,
and my laughter is denial.
While I'm sucking up the tears
that I hide behind a smile.
A painted face of happiness,
and outwardly I'm fine,
with a pretence for my self-defence,
my camouflage, by design.
You'll ask me how I'm doing
and I'm always just okay,
because you can't see beyond the make up
and the smile will always stay.
But turn your back for just one second
I'll allow to myself to choke,
on the desperate need I have to cry,
being the joker, is just no joke.

FLYERS AND FALLERS

I've stood shoulder to shoulder with giants,
I've been knocked off my feet by the breeze.
I've won and I've lost all my gambles,
I've flown high, and been brought to my knees.
I've faltered, I've failed, and I've fallen,
I've become, I've beaten and I've bled.
I've fought every fight that fate fed me,
and lost both my heart and my head.
Somewhere there's a sinner still winning,
deep in hell, an angel is lost.
There's some, free riding through this life,
and others, stuck, paying the cost.
We're each of us, flyers and fallers,
the broken, the brazen, the brave.
We're winners we're losers, we're lovers,
all lost and found souls, yet to save.

BE MY ANGEL

Take me from self torture,
for I'm more than all I seem.
Wrapped in blankets of regrets,
that still visit me, in dreams.
Come find me in my limbo,
wake me from the dead,
lift me with your gifts
of all those feelings that I dread.
Give to me a spark,
resurrect this fallen soul,
love the very pain of me,
help this broken heart, be whole.
Anoint my bleeding wounds,
and care for my despair,
blow the dust off my crumbling bones,
send it flying through the air.
Free me from my misery,
and guide me from the past,
show to me the road
away from shadows I have cast.
Be my remedy, be my reason,
be patient but be strong.
Be the angel that destroys my hell,
to prove my demons wrong.

Madness and Therapy

THE AFFAIR

A lack lustre lover becomes just another,
excuse for desires, to discover another.
With vacant eyes, and gilded tongue lies,
a picture is painted, a wolf in disguise.
Walks away from the cold, of the hands that he holds
to chase the desire, of a fire to unfold.
His impish grin to hide his sin,
the gentleman outwardly, devil within.
The touch of two souls, together now whole,
a spark that emits, from the moments they stole.
A burning inferno ensues and consumes
as piloted passions, dive in darkening rooms.
Bodies collide like supernova in skies,
that have failed to be lit by a cold lover's eyes.
The taboo, of these two, takes not an inch but a mile
as animal urgency, has no doubt or denial.
Every touch, every taste, every breath, every beat,
locked limbed lovers, are fuelled in this fantasy feat.
Pursuers of passions, mind and body connects,
lust driven to quivers of trembling wrecks.
Murmurs and mentions of secrets to keep,
red faced and breathless, with clothes in a heap.
Emotionless energy, returns as they leave,
back to the blankets of who they deceive.

STAY

Love yourself enough to stay
when others choose to leave.
See your reason among the ruins
that grants you time to breathe.
Learn to swim against, the raging tides,
when you feel that you could drown.
And lift yourself above it all
as the weight tries to pull you down.
Find the faith in you, that fate itself
is delivering this pain,
to learn lessons from the let downs,
so that you won't be hurt again.
See the great in your reflection
though the mirror may be broken,
and hear the words around you,
that all true friends have spoken.
Let the positive, persist,
watch negatives flow away.
And when others choose to leave you,
love yourself enough to stay.

IT'S OK

it's ok to feel lost
when you're already home
it's ok to feel lonely
when you are not alone
it's ok to let a tear fall
when you don't know why you cry
it's ok to have no answers
when you ask yourself "why?"
it's ok to miss yourself
when you don't know where you've been
it's ok to hurt inside
when the pain cannot be seen
it's ok to feel broken
when the fixers try their best
it's ok to stop a while
and admit you need a rest
it's ok, the discontent
when you're surrounded by your dreams
it's ok to be confused
when all is really as it seems
it's ok not to share your thoughts
as you hide yourself away
it's ok to feel just as you do
trust me,
it's all ok

TALKING IN OUR SLEEP

I'm buried in my own head,
under thoughts that run so deep,
yet here we are with eyes closed,
just talking in our sleep.
And we're waiting, just waiting,
to get down to the core,
of how we're really feeling,
of how we just want more.
We're lost in a forest of small talk,
and we just can't see the wood for the trees,
your hand in mine, too loose now, to lift me
when I fall once again to my knees.
The conversations we don't have, stay unheard.
Silenced by the sound of your sighs,
seeking what used to inspire you,
through your unrecognisable eyes.
The magic, the mayhem, the chaos,
the spark and the fires, all lost.
The days come and go without sunshine
as our souls are consumed by the frost.
We're just lying, to ourselves again
each afraid now, to go too deep.
And we're walking around with our eyes closed,
while we're talking all day, in our sleep.

PLAYLISTS

I'm listening to each lyric
of the songs we used to play,
and I'm lost inside the memory
of the words you'd always say.
The vibe of every playlist,
is loudly echoing echo your name,
while my heart just keeps on wondering
if it will ever be the same.
I'm not suffering with regret
and I don't wish to return,
to the place where we thought that
the fires would always burn.
Time is of the essence
and the essence here has gone,
but the smile creeps back upon my face,
with the words to every song.
Nostalgia is an enemy
but sometimes, it's a friend,
as happiness of how it started
is drowning out the end.
Maybe it never worked
for as long as we'd supposed
and maybe I took the drug of love,
and simply overdosed.
The days keep coming, the sun still shines
and night-time brings new dawns,
Angel wings never lose their flight,
when caught on devils horns.
We each did wrong, we each did right,
we each changed just like the weather,
and the happy ever after,
it seems was not forever.
But here we are in separate worlds
which once were destined to collide,

and though painful, we each still have
happy thoughts we cannot hide.
Thank God for you, and the miracle
of the moments shared in time,
and the pain of leaving, overshadowed,
knowing you were mine.
Moving on is never easy
and new roads come with some fear,
but I'll always look back fondly,
at the times that you were here.

RAINBOWS

she had so much light
inside of her,
that when
she danced in the rain,
she left rainbows
in her wake.

Madness and Therapy

IF THE SEEDS I PLANT STOP GROWING

I wrote a million letters
then burned each and every one,
couldn't speak the words out loud
to tell you how you did me wrong.
I'm not looking for excuses,
when I sometimes forget to try,
but if the seeds I plant stop growing,
I won't stay to watch them die.
I'll drive through all the red lights,
head for a place I've never been,
wipe away your memory
like the rain on my windscreen.
And I give the best advice
at 2 am, on my phone,
to any fool who cares to listen,
but I just can't take my own.
I'm not looking for excuses,
When I sometimes forget to try,
but if the seeds I plant stop growing,
I won't stay to watch them die.
And I know the futures smaller now
than all those wasted years,
where I set the world on fire
while I drowned in my own tears.
I'm not looking for excuses,
when I sometimes forget to try,
but if the seeds I plant stop growing,
I won't stay to watch them die.

POWER IN THE PAIN

There's two types of people, in the world today,
some have time for you, and others just won't stay.
and you're still believing as they are leaving
each and every word, they used to say,
you've been cursed at, for the worst of you
and praised when at your best,
chastised, for living lies
while pinning medals, to your chest.
And everything you ever took,
you took them, to extremes
and only found yourself existing
in the corners of your dreams.
You've got the same two arms, and hands
as anyone, you've ever met,
but what you've built with them, fell apart
and now you're broken, don't forget,
that there's magic, in the tragedy,
and there's power in your pain,
to take the rubble, from the ruins,
and carve your masterpiece again.

MEET THE REAL ME

Do you really know me?
If the smile is all you see.
And do you really feel me?
If you think I'm happy just to be.
Have you ever looked at me?
If you've never seen a tear.
Have you ever listened?
If you don't know what I fear.
Have you ever stood beside me?
If you think that I don't fall.
Have you ever walked with me?
If you've never watched me crawl.
You think that I'm the person,
that I allow the world to see,
well come and hold my empty hand a while,
And meet the real me.

MY SPARK

I guess I'm just a fool
who loses sight in sentiment,
and drowns, in the depths
of each "I love you" that is sent.
I keep getting lost in thoughts of you
and my head won't let you go,
as I dream and wish that "forever"
is the only future that we'll know.
My eyes meet yours, and then you steal
the next beat of my heart,
and my memory takes me for a walk
from now, back to the start.
There's a way to go, there's the moment now
there's the road down which we've been,
there's yesterday, there's tomorrow
and every today shared in-between.
There just seems to be this driving force
to push me on, or pull me through,
and it's the fire, alight, inside my soul
since the spark that came from you.

THE GIRL THAT HAS IT ALL

Every day is a battle, that she faces,
and she does so with a smile on her face,
she's a mixture of calamity and calm,
the perfect balance of chaos and of grace.
She has a soulful beauty like no other,
she has a heart, that's been broken, but still pure,
she will give, every moment that she's breathing,
while taking for herself, nothing more.
She can heal and can nurture with her presence,
and in her absence, her love is always felt,
she is the power within others to keep going,
even when the bad hands have been dealt.
There are no chinks of weakness in her armour,
though she's soft enough to let a tear fall,
she is an angel who has put to rest her demons,
she's just the girl, that really has it all.

DON'T SAY A WORD

I see your smile is fading baby,
I don't know why?
I swore that I would love you,
until the day I die.
I'd hold you when you'd close your eyes,
and tell you I was true,
catch you every time you fell,
my heart beats just for you.
Your heart don't feel so warm now,
your eyes have lost their glow,
reaching out to hold your hand,
I can feel you letting go.
I think of when our souls were one,
go back to the start,
but paths, they run their course in life,
and now's the time to part.
Turn before you leave the door,
and everything we shared,
that look in your eyes, holds all the goodbyes,
so please don't say a word.

MY SISTER

Turn the clock back,
make those moments last,
the good times rolled,
but they disappeared too fast,
every second counted more, than we ever could have known.
And somewhere, in all the in-betweens,
in the "should have dones",
and those "might have beens"
are the times we failed to see, would soon have flown.

It's a cruel world that, would take away,
a chance again, for me to say,
I miss you, and I wish you, all the best.
I saw your eyes closed, I was hoping,
that you'd wake up, and they would open,
but I guess, it was just your time, to rest.
I'll say goodbye, every day, inside my head,
pretend we took back, every bad thing said,
and I'll think of, the best times, and not the bad.
There was only one you, never be another,
I'm a grown man now, but still your little brother,
If only we knew, what little time, we had.

Turn the clock back,
make those moments last,
the good times rolled,
but they disappeared too fast,
every second counted more, than we ever could have known.
And somewhere,
in all the in-betweens,
in the "should have dones",
and those "might have beens"
are the times we failed to see, would soon have flown.

HIATUS

Filled with thoughts that overflow,
and as emotion bursts the dam,
hectic head and hurried heartbeats,
fuels the foolish man I am.
A myriad of mindful musings,
sentimental sparks that speak,
notions that could fill oceans,
yet the words that come are weak.
In empathy of emptiness,
my inspiration, dark and dank,
poignancy eludes my pen,
and the page before me, blank.
What flows, will come and I await,
like the rising moon calling the tide,
and the screwed-up balls of paper,
the only evidence that "I've tried".
I conclude my mind is clouded,
yet I think, I feel, I look,
and although hiatus haunts me
I'm never a closed book.

Madness and Therapy

TO THE WIRE

Hey there, do you know me by name?
Or do you see me as another,
who maybe feels the same?
A road less travelled,
and yet here we are again,
walking there together,
so far away from where we came.

Taking no heed in the warnings, and ignoring every sign.
I'm going to take it to the wire, this time.

I took my doubts as my disciples,
you've got demons as your friends.
Salvation found in solitude,
we're beginning, where it ends.
Shoulders sodden from salt water,
that has fallen from your eyes,
the bruises worn upon your heart,
from another lovers lies.

And yet I take no heed in the warnings, I'm ignoring every sign.
I'm going to take it to the wire, this time.

We've found that certain something,
in the midst of losing all.
Pride may have come before,
but faith is following the fall.
The odds were stacked against,
those who had loved and lost,
and once rich in pure emotion,
now broke from all it cost.

But here I'm taking no heed in warnings, ignoring every sign.
I'm going to take it to the wire, this time.

THE DEVILS CUP

I sold my soul to the devil just last Friday,
and the gates to my heaven, they have closed.
Took temptation and gambled with the future,
my angels and my demons juxtaposed.
I raised a glass, to the souls of long forgotten,
I danced to the dread of sweet regret.
I sang in silence to the melody of mayhem,
with open arms to friends I've not yet met.
Each tomorrow will bring new ways to haunt me,
as my yesterdays keep slipping from my grip.
I close my eyes and dream away the present,
and from the devil's cup I'll take another sip.

ECLIPSE

My heart, eclipsed, and love was black,
in my shade, I wished for light,
but you sat with me, in my darkness,
until morning chased the night.

DAWNING LOVE

Time has passed me by
in the blink of an eye
and I've shouldered burdens, no man should ever hold.
I've been to the bottom
a soul long lost, forgotten
no winning hand, and losing dice were rolled.
And I've doubted my existence
held value to another
and my heart was crumbling, without notice, into dust.
A smile, gone, lost in despair
open eyes, with vacant stare
a reflection in the mirror, I couldn't trust.
Then as I was throwing in my hand
whilst losing the strength to stand
through the darkness, of my everlasting night.
Came a glimpse of brighter morning
as a love inside was dawning
and you walked in, and brought with you the light.
There's damage, this we're knowing
and no promise of where we're going
but just take my hand, and together we may see.
That the lessons life has taught
through the battles we have fought
deserve this love that's come, it's fate, it's destiny.

DO NOT JUST BE

Do not just be,
do not exist as a feather on the wind,
as a ripple in the lake,
as the leaf,
amongst a million more,
in amber carpets of autumn.
Do not just be,
draw your inferno from within,
and raze restriction into ashy ground.
Blow your hurricane,
obliterate obstinate opposition in the eye of your storm.
Become the tempestuous tsunami
of your ties.
Do not just be,
do not suppress your chaos,
dream chaser, storm racer, trail blazer.
Let it be known that you were here,
life is a waste of living
if we live it, waiting to die.

RESURRECT

Take your high head of hopes
that delusion is erased
with a reason for believing,
as illusion is replaced.
There's only fine lines to cross
and only mole hills left to climb,
when eyes are now re opened
to the mountains by design.
There's no fear again of falling
through the floor of imposed doubts,
and there's no silence to a whisper
now louder than those muted shouts.
The fragility, placed within
took hits, and there, not broken,
as the bullets of deception
just leave yourself awoken.
Standing taller than the weight allowed,
the burden of neglect,
recognise again, your mirror view
and embrace your resurrect.

SURVIVAL

There is electric in the air today
and I inhale deeply
savouring the flavour of survival.
My mind spiralling
thoughts awash with positivity
good memories stored like trinkets,
priceless gems that cannot be stolen.
Locked in a safe that cannot be cracked
and the bad... the bad memories
I toss them into the fires
burning them to fuel my onward path
knowing that without that fuel
and without those gems
I'd have nothing.
And I am here now, with everything,
and I am now everything
because of, and in spite of
each win and every loss.
And that my friend
is survival.

ROYAL ROMANCE

Let's take a walk this night, just you and I,
along an astral plane,
while supernovas serenade
and the moon begins to wane.
Let's take each star as a guiding light,
from which our souls can't hide
and send comets racing through the universe
when our galaxies collide.
Let's use the blanket sky above us,
as a dancefloor of our own
where the planets all line up
to teach the steps that lead us home.
A syncopated salsa,
in the space that lives between
reality and dream worlds
where I'm your King, and you're my Queen.

A HUNDRED FEET TALL

My defences made sense
of each fake friends pretence.
Those who smile and attack
with a knife in my back,
sucker punching my pride
while they hunt me in packs.
Ain't no sympathy symphony,
these are the facts.
I took every beating
and rolled with the whacks.
I say a fuck you, now
to those sewer rats.
Got my life on the tracks,
I never look back.
Strive forwards to chances,
take no backwards glances,
where others would fall
never once did I stall
I took every stone
that they threw and built walls.
Which I climbed, up above them
to look down and call,
"Look at me mother fuckers,
I'm a hundred feet tall."

FOOLS GOLD

Just where do you start
when you question your beginning
about the moments that you lost
when you thought that you were winning.
Though the endings never reached
of the rainbow, you still find,
that you have chased a pot of fools gold
around the wishes in your mind.
Trying to catch the bubbles
of your dreams, they burst too soon
and yet you find you're reaching stars,
while you're shooting for the moon.
There's an up with every downward turn
and with every fall, there is a flight,
there's a cheekbone smile with each denial
with every shadow, there's a light.
For every empty, there's a thimble full,
with each silence, there's still singing.
It falls apart, back to the start,
the answer's still, at your beginning.

MOON BEAMS

She talks of catching moon beams
as though that's where magic can occur,
but I've witnessed the truly magical
when the moon beams, are catching her.

SINGE

Kiss me
with the passion
that calms the storm within.
Fan my flames
with angel wings
and I'll singe them with my sin.

IN THE STORM

So many times I have changed
to become the person that they
wanted to love, to fit into the
shape of their missing piece.
So many times I have lost myself
by becoming moulded into an
unrecognisable version of who
I'm not.
And then I question why
hearts break and love leaves,
why words fall to the pavement
like rain, flooding the gutters
and disappearing down the drain
of the forgotten.
Then I catch my reflection in a
puddle and think...I remember you.
This time, my arms are held wide,
my mouth is open, drinking the
downpour of everything you tell
me, while I remain unchanged, and
I feel you falling in love,
with who I am in the storm.

HEADS OR TAILS

Do I, don't I
Shall I, shan't I
Would I, will I
Can I, can't I
Upside, downside
Inside, out
Less than, more than
Belief and doubt
Brim full, empty
Solid, hollow
Silence, echoes
Yesterday
Tomorrow
Safe, danger
Real, disguise
Open, honest
Bare faced lies
Is it, isn't it
Build and break
Smile, cry
True, fake
Kill, cure
Master, beginner
Head and heart
Saint or sinner

Madness and Therapy

PIPE DREAMS AND LULLABIES

If there's an angel on my shoulder,
then surely, she must see,
the sands of time are shifting,
as the winds of change blow free.

Kept a promise, shared a secret,
spoke the truth, I heard a lie,
stole a moment, but gave no reason,
saved a life, for a chance to say goodbye.

Pipe dreams and lullaby's,
rocky roads, and rainbow skies,
first hellos and long goodbyes,
one love found, and another one dies.
Pain deceit and lies,
wipe the tears from your eyes
just take what fate denies,
pipe dreams and lullabies.

Never played it safe,
forgot to hedge my bets,
left no time, to toe the line,
or deal with my regrets,
journeyed with the reaper,
fuelled by my desire,
spread my wings as I fly,
then take each high much higher

My head is full of dreams,
that never let me sleep.
Living like a playboy,
but buying on the cheap.
I know the inch is mine,
but I'll always steal a mile,

Madness and Therapy

juggling with sanity,
but hell it makes me smile.
I'm on a never-ending search,
for self-satisfaction.
All plans fall by the wayside,
I'm driven by distraction.
I'm falling off a wagon,
that's losing all its wheels,
a helter skelter ride to hell,
but I love the way it feels,

Pipe dreams and lullaby's,
rocky roads, and rainbow skies,
first hellos and long goodbyes,
one love found, and another one dies.
Pain deceit and lies,
wipe the tears from your eyes
just take what fate denies,
pipe dreams and lullabies.

Kept a promise, shared a secret,
spoke the truth, I heard a lie,
stole a moment, but gave no reason,
saved your life, for a chance to say goodbye.

Pipe dreams and lullaby's,
rocky roads, and rainbow skies,
first hellos and long goodbyes,
one love found, and another one dies.
Pain deceit and lies,
wipe the tears from your eyes
just take what fate denies,
pipe dreams and lullabies.

Madness and Therapy

SERIAL SPILLER

An epiphany, occurred to me,
that words were all you shared with me.
My reality, a waste of me, descending to calamity.
Plummet from the summit of the world I built for all to see,
I ache, wide awake, raking up past mistakes,
to validate what's at stake, and to risk my own fate.
My opinion, a vision, I voiced by decision
if they'd listen, my mission to maintain my position,
to show matter of factly that I'll keep intact
my integrity, primarily, (a tactic I lacked).
Would just shine, like a beacon that's mine,
a flashlight of what's right, without reason to fight.
But Giving way to the weight of the great understaters,
a checkmate of fate, anticipated by haters,
by the lies in their eyes, that were taught to despise.
Fuelling the flames, with Chinese whisper games,
I opened my heart to pave way for the start,
and emitting emotion, I'm spitting explosions.
A notion of oceans of love and devotion.
Creating a space, to finally trace,
my steps taken before, in this forsaken place.
Forgotten in rotten downtrodden despair,
a problem so modern, that nobody cares.
Listing what's missing, I spotlight the cause,
put myself centre stage, but that just started wars.
Never intentionally disrupting harmony,
stating my case, to prevent inner harm to me.
The slings and the arrows that flew at my plight,
like emotional marksmen, who had me in sight.
A heart is a target once exposed to nail,
with bullets of bitter, and bombs of betrayal.
Should've put up and shut up, but up and away,
the thoughts grew their wings, and flew with each one I'd say.
Guilty of hoping that openness finds,

to be seen as a strength, not a weakness of kinds.
I act only in kindness, but portrayed as a killer
speaking my sentiments, a serial spiller.

The Art Of Letting Go

The more they let you down
the less that you expect,
the less they then deliver
and the less you will accept.

YOU'VE GOT THIS

You can do it, you know you can.
You've done it before.
You've picked up the fragmented pieces from the
destruction that left you broken, you've rebuilt
yourself and stood tall again, held your head
high and silenced all the doubters.
You've climbed to the peak, from the very bottom,
even when you feel you've drawn your last breath.
Proving to yourself that you and only you, hold the
power to persist and have enough self-worth to kick
the rubble aside and strive onwards.
You've sworn to yourself you'll never be there again,
never fall or falter... yet here you are once more,
knocked to the floor.
They say don't look back at the past, to focus on
the future but I say no, I say look back, look behind you,
look at all the times that you've risen and that you've
flown again into success.
Look longingly at how no blows from before have ever
kept you down.
Observe your power and realise, believe, and have faith
in the evidence that you've got this strength inside.
Now embrace it, harness it, and use it to fuel yourself once
more to get back onto your feet.
You can do it, you know you can.
You've done it before.
Now you're doing it again.
You've got this.

THE VOID

The clock, becomes my enemy
I watch the stars fade in the skies,
and I lay beside, your empty space
as the sun fights the moon to rise.
I just wish that I could turn back time,
as every tick, brings new regret,
of how my demons seem to scream your name,
and of the love I can't forget.
I see your outline in the shadows
so I pray that light won't shine,
to keep me here in my midnight,
because tomorrow you're not mine.
If I could just get more time to dream
of how I'd tell your soul what it should hear,
that I'd hold you tight forever
so each morning you're still here.
I reach across the void you've left
I feel that space too, in my heart,
watching seconds ticking forwards
no way to turn, back, to the start.

BEFORE THE STORM

There is a time, that came before
they inflicted hurt, left her raw,
before they silenced, all she'd spoken
and crushed her soul, left her heart broken.
A time exists, when she could be
open, true, wild, and free.
Before the storm, before the rain
before the tears and before the pain,
before she built her fortress high
with solid walls, that reach the sky.
She wears a mask, and hides behind
a steely soul, titanium mind,
she's bulletproof, and won't reveal
the emotion only she can feel.
She's a little lost, from all she'd been
makes sure her weakness, can't be seen,
life gave her lessons, made her stronger
almost who she was, no longer.
Her eyes they show, the true soft side
that's kept away, since she denied
herself to miss, the things she'd lack
and to that time, she will get back.

MOON SECRETS

Her worries taunt her sleepless night
and though they don't consume,
you'll find her sharing secrets
through her window to the moon.
The stars shining up above her,
like glitter in the sky,
turn each worry into wishes
to put the sparkle in her eye.
And even though sleep will escape her
and morning comes with no real hurry,
there's a new day fast approaching
to take away her every worry.

WANTS IN A LIFETIME

I want to see the angels,
but I never learned to fly.
I want to go to heaven,
but I just don't want to die.
I want to see the world,
from the comfort of my bed.
While sitting in the silence
of the words I never said.

A LITTLE DARKNESS

The sun's going down on history
and I've learned to look away.
Let horizons hide, what's been and gone
and instead live just for today.
There's a thousand smiling faces
coming out to greet the night,
it's a promise of the morning
that's displayed by candlelight.
And all of us are stars,
we're just trying to shine again,
and we each need a little darkness
to find another shining friend.

LONELY EYES

The stars may mask, for all that look
the darkness of the skies,
and hidden, in the shadows
falls the tear, from lonely eyes.
They dare not tell you how they feel
for fear of emotion that turns sour,
like the planting of a seed
that with no sunlight, will not flower.

THE MIRROR MAN

As I look into my mirror
at the eyes that stare right back,
I see the look of disgust
at everything I lack.
My mirror man, he lets me know
without ever speaking out,
that I do not meet his measure
of a view he likes to doubt.
And I just seek his approval
a gentle nod, maybe a smile,
Show something, damn reflection
that makes me feel worthwhile.
My helter skelter head takes me
down some rabbit hole,
where I will never look or be
what others see as whole,
Inferiority, I think it's called
but it manifests itself much deeper,
into despising the man I am
just a solo, shadowed weeper.
Paranoia does not just creep in,
it tornadoes through my brain,
with thoughts of perfect others
and why I can't be the same.
It's an illness, yes, I know this,
but logic doesn't rule,
when demons ride emotion
through a mirror minded fool.
Take heed of this, and know
that those mirrors always lied,
never showing what we fail to see,
the true beauty deep inside.

REGRETS

I'm a little bit dead inside.
Lost the will, with every tear cried.
Said goodbye too many times, for just one lifetime.
I'm infected with dark memories,
the should have beens, of the deceased,
I let go with weakened hands, of all that's mine.
Heartbreak misery steals relief,
from melancholy, disbelief
Failed at being me, but God knows I was trying.
Pain just reminds me I exist,
Nostalgia hits with iron fist,
it seems I only felt alive when I was dying.

PLAYING WITH FIRE

do
not
douse
your flames
for anybody,
if they
burn
their fingers,
then they
shouldn't
have
played
with
fire.

BEAUTY IN THE BREAKAGE

I want to write about souls.
To compare them to blocks of marble,
I want to tell you that you shouldn't
spend your time, with someone who'll take
a Hammer and a chisel to yours,
chipping away at it, attempting to shape it
into what they want.
I want you to know that if yours isn't right
for them the way it is, that it never will be.
I want to write about how this happened to me,
mine, whittled into an unrecognisable shape,
surrounded by splinters of who I could have been.
I also want to say how a wonderful somebody,
came along and saw those pieces.
I didn't pay full attention to her collecting
them all, as I was feeling shapeless, lifeless, empty.
I want to find the words to describe how she lovingly
took each piece, and polished it, placed it
and arranged it into what I began to see, was no longer
cast away rubble, but was the beautiful mosaic of me.
I'll never find the words to make poetry of this.
It's too wonderful and complex.
She didn't fix me, but instead she showed me
that there's no shame in being broken.
She saw the beauty in my breakage
and I love her for it.

SMOKE AND MIRRORS

You'll never get to heaven,
with your feet on the ground,
because it's all smoke and mirrors,
til the walls come tumbling down.
Did you ever stop to wonder,
if there's a reason you can't find,
to the pain in your heart,
and the weight on your mind?
You've got to just slow down,
to let yourself breathe,
let your angels hold you,
while your demons leave.
Be open, to all,
of the good that lies ahead,
to fill your empty heart,
and to empty your full head.
Without taking the time,
just to, again, find yourself,
You'll remain, a prisoner,
to your suffering mental health.
So step on forwards, step on,
and face the rising sun,
Your journey, to be you again,
has only just begun.

ONE CHANCE

I've had to make sacrifices just to find myself,
and get lost in all the places that I'd roam.
I've had to say words that nobody would listen to,
and walk away from hearts that I called home.
I've made rivers from the tears that have fallen,
I've lost faith in all the truths that I knew,
I've been a stranger to the friends who surround me,
and let my pain be hidden from their view.
I've been taught all that glitters isn't golden,
I've learned that there's still more pain to feel,
I've become a better me despite falling,
far enough to learn just what was real.
There's highs and there's lows and there's learning,
there's smiles amid the pain of being true,
there's a never-ending journey just to give yourself,
the only chance, you've ever got, of being you

Madness and Therapy

16/05/2020

You heard the news today,
but you can't feel the way I do.
Building bridges as the island
slowly disappears from view.
Too little too late,
is what they always say,
I heard it, but never felt it,
until the darkness hit today.
In melancholy memory,
my tears have no place to land,
now that my arms are open,
yet I cannot hold your hand.
Regret is a feeling that grips,
strangles the strongest mind,
starving hope like no breath to take,
and there's nothing you can find
to take away soulful hurt
and to remedy the pain,
of knowing there's no chance left,
to say sorry once again.

AMOR FATI

There's a place or time...
actually, there is a place, *and,* a time,
that only exist in one moment. For each
and every person it may be different.
Mine is here. This very spot, This very moment.
The now, that ceases to be, just as you begin
to realise that you're in it.
The here, that can alter before your eyes,
as colours, lights, and shadows change.
I love the water. The wind off the coast.
The time of day that's not quite dusk, and the sun
is not yet ready to set.
That to me is the moment to sit and reflect.
Insignificant factors fade, and what's
important rises to the surface.
I suppose a religious person, might call this prayer.
But, to me...
all my questions get answered as the day is put
to rest, and the elements vocalise your emotions.
A soft echo of all that has been, but a calming whisper,
of all that's yet to come.
Serene.
This, right here, right now. Is my moment.
And, for a fleeting second,
the world makes sense.

A WHISPER TO AN ANGEL

I stripped the meat from my bones
so I could bare them all to you,
and I see you, in your weakness, do the same.
A give and take of fears
and a vulnerable display,
that proves to one another, it's no game.
There's a haunting from the past,
a ghost that visits in the dark,
a stark reminder, that some wounds, will never heal.
But I'm casting light in your direction,
and I'm holding on so tight,
trying to convince you, that the monsters, are not real.
I wish to build a future
from broken shards of your past,
though some pieces, may hurt my hands to hold.
But I promise you I'll try,
even if it bleeds me dry,
to keep the fears away, that make your heart turn cold.
Every morning that I wake
before my eyes, greet the day,
you're the thought that fills the plans within my head.
And as I'm about to sleep.
before I let my dreams take me,
you're the silent prayer inside my soul that I have said.

IT'S ALL YOU

It's that smile that makes my world complete,
it's that voice that calms my storm,
it's that touch that takes the cold away,
and makes my heart feel warm.
It's that moment when I hear the laugh,
that silences my sighs,
it's the faith and hope that comes my way
from looking in those eyes.
It's the knowing that I'm not alone,
no matter just how far away
those arms are from holding me,
that gets me through the day.
it's the pure and truthful words that come,
when demons are whispering to me,
it's the light that takes the darkness,
and enables me to see.
it's the one and only certainty,
that I can carry through
it's the single thing that reaffirms my faith,
and my darling, it's all you.

ONE MAN BAND

You are my drug of choice
and I have overdosed.
I bared my bones to you
but now you're just a ghost.
You'd helped me brick by brick
to dismantle all my doubt.
I escaped my walls, into your heart
now I can't find my way out.
You helped me, to stand
when all I could do was fall,
now left with just memories,
like you were never here at all.
I was finally complete,
my puzzle pieces, fit your own,
the picture's once again fragmented
now you've left me all alone.
I'm just a disaster walking
as life fails to play my tune,
a syncopated sadness
as the music ends too soon.
There is no encore to this performance
now my hand's not in your hand,
because love is an orchestra
and I'm just a one man band.

PILLOW TALK

You're having a tough old time of it
and the thoughts inside your head weigh you down.
Emotion hits you like a tidal wave
and you feel that you could drown.
With every effort that you put in
and in every way you try,
you just can't seem to please them all
and your heart beats with a sigh.
No one can see, and nobody knows
and you choose to never share,
for fear of being misconstrued
you're silent, because you care.
And you rest your head at night-time
only your pillow knows you weep,
as you close your eyes until tomorrow
to let your tears sleep.

WEARY EYES

In the aftermath
of chaos
stood amid the
ruins of my past,
lost inside
the darkness,
of the shadow
I have cast.
The sun dances over
clouded skies, towards the moon,
and night-time follows day,
as time passes all too soon.
Caged within the confines
of a heart that beat in sighs,
a dank and lifeless soul,
looking out through
weary eyes.

FRAN

I cherish moments that I spent,
as Summers came, and Winters went,
with memories and sentiment,
that first blown kiss, to you was sent.
From baby boy, to teen, to man,
from crawling then, to as I stand,
I placed my lips, upon my hand,
I blew you kisses and watched them land.
Gone too soon, no reason why,
with heavy heart and teary eye
I'll tilt my head up to the sky,
and blow you one last kiss goodbye.

PERFECTION TO MY PASSIONS

I don't know if she can hear me
when the stresses of the day
drown out the sound of every word
that my heart is trying to say
and maybe she can't see me
when she's so deep inside her mind
weighed down by heavy thoughts
that it almost makes her blind
I wonder if she knows though
that I'll wait and guard a while
all the reasons that she still has
to wear her gorgeous smile
because even when the days are tough
and when she feels she can't cope
I hold enough faith for two of us
and I hang on to her hopes
She's perfection to my passions
her soul is made to measure
to fit so well beside my own
and her smile is my treasure

LET'S GET SOME AIR

I caught that look you threw my way,
then you watched me smiling back,
and every time our eyes met time stood still.
I try to find the words that may
take you home tonight,
but deep inside I know I never will.
I'd love to walk across to you and ask you for a dance,
then I'd take your hand and lead you to the floor
and in my imagination, I would say 'let's get some air',
then together we would step towards the door.
Because the girl has got me crazy
though I never knew her name,
but in my sleep I'm calling out for her.
I never heard her voice and yet
she's singing in my dreams,
a melody that slowly fills the air.
But looking back and wishing
I had swept you off your feet,
and together disappeared into the sun.
Knowing that my life
would always be so incomplete,
should've held your hand and told you 'you're the one'.
But a memory of you my dear
as small as it may be,
is enough to light up each and every day
and looking back I swear its true,
regret, it fills my soul,
and I wish I never turned and walked away.
I'd love to walk across to you and ask you for a dance,
then I'd take your hand and lead you to the floor.
And in my imagination, I would say 'let's get some air',
then together we would step towards the door.

THE SMILES AND THE SIGHS

She's been known to move mountains with no effort,
she's met herself coming back again, some days.
She's everything to everybody, but no one to herself,
and she's not, as ok, as what she says.
She's happy, but she's tired of never stopping,
there's more to her that she will let you see.
She is mother, she is lover, she's a goddess of a girl,
but her identity seems lost in memory.
She sometimes needs, but a moment, just to be herself again,
she sometimes, just needs to close her eyes.
She sometimes doesn't know if it's time to laugh or cry,
when she gets lost between the smiles and the sighs

STRONG

Being strong doesn't mean
being unaffected by it all,
it means walking towards
your destination with tear
soaked cheeks and a heart
as heavy as lead.

BALLOON HEART

The best way I can describe it, is that you can't burst an "empty" balloon.
Much like the human heart. The more love, care, compassion, empathy, and sympathy that you fill it with, the more inflated it becomes.
It expands, stretches, and grows into something so beautiful that everybody wants to touch it. It draws people to it, this huge balloon heart of yours, and it attracts every person that has it in their focus.
The more you put in, the more that it continues to grow, and yet the more it holds, the lighter it gets, floating effortlessly and beautifully though this world.
It is a magnificent feeling to have a heart that is in this condition, and you reach a state of ultimate bliss during those moments that it is filled with so much positive emotion.

But then all it takes...

is one fucking prick.

WEAR YOUR CROWN

Your crown may become tarnished,
a result of all that you've been through,
and what once sat proudly gleaming
sits dullened and askew.
Each battle you have beaten,
each torment along the way,
every single tear that's fallen,
and the scars that you display.
They're each a trophy of your wonder,
a prize to proudly keep,
amongst the flowers that have been watered
to grow each time you weep.
You're the hero in your story,
every chapter, every verse,
and the fact you still wear a crown at all,
shows you're unbeaten by your curse.
It's time to look upon the ruins
of the times your castle fell,
and you picked up each piece of rubble
to build a bridge out of your hell.
You're here now and standing proud
with a tale, choosing to share it,
about how the power is not within the crown,
but in those that choose to wear it.

YOUR WINGS

There's more to being human, than just hurting.
Pain can become the substance, of each day.
When the lips that said I love you, say goodbye now,
and it's harder now to stay, than walk away.
Stars don't stop shining in the daytime,
they just hide away and wait again for night.
Unseen, it feels that they're forgotten,
as someone else has come along to steal their light.
It's time to let me go, but leave me flying,
be on your way, but first, please cut my strings.
Let me soar now, here, in my solitude,
sometimes it's heartbreak, that gives to you, your wings

CALMING INFLUENCE

Just as I was about
to rage war against
my demons,
she kissed each one,
and gave them
the wings they needed
to fly away.

Madness and Therapy

I DON'T MIND

I don't mind the not knowing
I don't mind the wait and see
I don't mind the need to wait,
to first take care of history.
I don't have a need for now
to answer queries that I find,
have previously misled me
by messing with my mind.
There's a certain satisfaction
of just knowing that a day,
can twist the hand of fate
and send a smile or two my way.
I walked away, to the find the me
that another had kept hidden,
self-doubt and negativity
both quickly overridden.
Now what will be, will be
and what was not, was not,
and my positivity returns to me
with the man I had forgot.

TIME AND SPACE

Please don't dwell so long in silence
that shadows come into your mind,
and listen to your heartbeat
not to the voices they may find.
Rest a while, alone, that's healthy,
find your place that brings you calm.
But do not hide, if you are hiding with
the thoughts that can bring harm.
Alone is never lonely
when you take with you all your light,
but if your solitude brings self neglect,
you can lose yourself to night.
I will wait until you return,
give you time and space to grow.
But if I sense you're lost inside the darkness
I will join you until you glow.

Madness and Therapy

FAREWELL FRIEND

I'm mad at you for leaving me
I need to scream that to your face,
and that there's no other, now, or never
would fit in to this empty space.
We were supposed to take this world by storm
and to anybody who would ask,
just what the hell we think we're doing,
we'd tell to kiss our ass.
I'm tough enough for two of us
and yet now that you have gone,
I feel I'm looking for my other half
and not strong enough for one.
I'm going to miss you for a lifetime,
I knew your soul like it was mine,
I could rely on you and trust you
and no matter, we'd be fine.
You had my back, I had yours
and our fires raged together,
not one thing could keep us down
it should've been that way forever.
My greatest friend, my true soul mate,
my counterpart in all to be,
you were supposed to be right here
and now it's only me.
We're two sides of the same coin,
we're two halves that make a whole,
so the grief is fucking hard to bear
now that my sidekick has been stole.
No-one will understand the depth,
nobody ever will,
time will never heal this wound
in years I'll feel it still.
I'm mad with you for leaving me,
but I'm grateful that we met

and every step I take without you
I promise I'll not forget.

OLD ROMANTICS

The old romantics state
that they would
"lay down and die for you",
but her hand slips into mine,
she sees the value in me
as she stares into my soul,
makes me feel worthwhile,
and all I can think is
"I'd stand up and live for you"

GRIEF

Grief is a dirty
bar room brawler.
You can be
sat there
minding your own business
drinking
or laughing
or both
and then bang
along he comes,
punching you in the kidneys
just to remind you
that you'd
stopped paying attention
to him
for just one second.

BIG SURPRISE

No remedy, pretend to me
you never were a friend to me.
It's plain to see, insanity
causes your calamity.
I'm choosing to be losing you
breaking bones not bruising you,
I'm flying high not cruising through,
one digit, I'm Saluting you.
Above you not below you now,
your own lies overthrow you now.
I'll show the world your over now,
you're love drunk, I'm hungover now.
You lingered much too long,
to be ringing true the wrong
of the words sung to your song
and all along, you don't belong.
So be gone, so be gone.
In the memory of all I see,
the hazy craziness of me,
losing all reality,
due to heard words of the miss with me.
No mystery, that she would be
no more than a bitch to me,
a shadow in my history.
Good riddance all she is to me,
a better man alone you'll see.
Rise above the lies,
dodging lows and taking highs,
open up all of their eyes,
as they see through your disguise.
A word now to the wise,
the truth never denies
as each lie of me now dies
I'm back now, big surprise!

THE GIRL WHO GREW TOO FAST

She's the girl who saw too much, too young
she's the girl who grew too fast,
the girl who placed all others first
while counting herself last.
She's the girl who life forgot it seems,
and the girl who was denied
the chance to live naively
and to remain the child inside.
She cares for all her hand can reach,
she feels all that she can see,
she fills empty hearts with the love she has,
pure spirit, wild and free.
On the outside, you'll see stability
and you'll see balance and you'll see strength,
you'll see the woman grown, who would
save you at any length.
But deeper in that soul
if you care to look into the eyes,
the girl inside is still there
and she hides the fact she cries.
She sees in herself, low value
and she can't just seem to grow,
from the girl who needed holding more
and telling so she'd know.
That she was worth so much more to all,
that she should place herself above
the doubt she holds within her head,
and instead allow her to feel loved.
And her mirror would always tell her
that the woman who stares back,
is never quite going to be enough
and reflects everything she lacks.
She knows she should be worth more
than these demons let her feel,

she knows that the self doubt
and denial isn't real.
And she's fought the world to get here
and she's won each battle on the way,
strong woman stands before her now
in the mirrors new display.
She could so easily have given up
each time she'd been denied,
but the woman who grew too much too soon,
has fought to save the girl inside.

BITTERNESS

Some people just
chew you up.
Spit you out
when they've
had their fill,
then seek pity
complaining
about a bitter
taste left in their
mouths.

ONE MORE STEP

I lost myself in a moment
and maybe blinded by the stars,
wishing softly upon each one above
as I dared to show my scars.
I gave freely everything I am
and dreamed that I could see,
a tomorrow that was conjured
from the mists left behind me.
I was stripped bare and naked
and I handed my broken heart,
to hands I thought would keep it safe
but then watched them rip apart.
I came with damaged edges
and first saw through teary eyes,
the look that promised rescue
but instead wore a disguise.
And there's a wistful way in memory
that tore a hole in all I'd been,
as the mists began to slowly clear,
eyes open, the mask was seen.
I should've stepped more wisely,
should've listened to my head,
should've kept my walls much higher
and took care of me instead.
But regrets they do not feature
and I can't hold hatred in my day,
all things happen for a reason,
time for things to go my way.
And I'm seeing now tomorrow
is just one more step to go,
and there is a hand, now holding mine
and I won't be letting go.

MISS YOU DAYS

I find you in each lyric
as the radio sings,
I feel your soft kisses
in the warmth the sunlight brings.
I hear you in the slow,
rhythmic swaying of the trees,
the leaves whispering your name
while being met by the breeze.
My thoughts bring us both together
as dandelion wishes float on by,
my imagination has us dancing,
like the clouds across the sky.
Sunshine bounces off the water
and I see you in the haze,
just simple things, that bring you here,
on these, my "miss you" days.

Madness and Therapy

NARCISSIST HEART

My instincts driving, the future I survive in,
the strife cuts like a knife, in this game I'm losing life in.
Been cut, pretty much, to my core,
stuck in a rut, but what for,
gotta put up, or shut up,
gonna fight, I want more.
I've been weakened by words
as I speak, but not heard.
Hid my face, in this phase, a
tongue that stung like a razor
and I'm torn apart, from the start,
by a narcissist heart.
She's just playing a part
to simply destroy, the soul of the boy
as she's making fake love to, just make him her toy.
Had to race to a place
I could escape to at haste
and free from the shadows,
I first saw her face.
No denial, desire, had to have that embrace,
lifted higher, with fire, than the liar I'd faced.
And she opened my eyes,
saw right through my disguise,
and with angel wing heartbeats, she silenced my cries.
And I knew in that second the
future that beckons is her,
and despair is a care
I've left back in the past
and it has to stay there.
And she's holding my world
as I'm telling the heavens
this angel's my girl.

SMILES AND CRIES

I'm a dreamer
this I'm knowing,
with a fools imagination
my inner child's not growing.
A lover of the open,
a lover of the free,
my smiles, they outweigh my cries,
I'm a lover of love, you see.
My mood is up, more than it's down,
I've fought to feel this way.
I've gotten here through battles,
and faced demons day to day.
I've hidden deep in shadows past,
I've been hurt, and I've felt pain.
I've been rocked before, to my very core,
but I came back again.
I can throw my head back in the sun,
taste rain, falling from the skies.
I see beauty in most everything,
and my smiles outweigh my cries.
I can love and I can be loved,
a romantics heart, it beats inside.
and it's been no easy journey,
but I've smiled, more than I've cried.
I know we all have had our troubles,
and we struggle to feel free,
but I've reached a point, my mirror man,
is smiling back at me.

LOST YOUTH

Life gets wasted on the youth sometimes
and those that never get to grow,
leave an empty sadness
and from your eyes it's going to show.
Despite the paths we choose to walk
this life will always test,
and the tragedy has no justice
when youth is laid to rest.
The chance to watch the years pass by,
never given, all is lost,
wrong place, wrong time, wrong choices
and now they've paid the highest cost.
Sadness from each salted tear
and empty void within the heart,
each wish, never quite enough
to go back to the start.
But strength is found within your soul
to embrace the smiles you shared,
to celebrate each memory
with everyone who cared.
Grief strikes you so deep inside,
the wound will never heal,
but in that same place, the love you shared,
will always keep them real.
Your time still goes on without them,
you'll still walk your path in life,
and you'll get slowly to where you're going,
despite this carried strife.
Your eyes may leak, your heart may hurt
and though those feelings show,
you must raise your head to what's to come,
knowing you've still to grow.
Life is wasted on the youth sometimes
and the advice they'll always give,

is to learn to keep on going
because you've still got your life to live.

CAGED

You claimed to the world that
you loved me, then placed my
heart into a cage.
Forgetting to feed it,
and not giving it
room to grow,
while all the time wondering,
why it didn't sing
for you anymore.

THE LANGUAGE OF TWO LOVERS

You won't know where it comes from
and you won't know where it goes,
you won't know if they see it
because you don't know if it shows.
How the world ceases to exist
and sudden absence of all other,
and time forgets to move
in the presence of another.
There's a spark that cannot be described
and hope breathes against once more,
as passion wakes a sleeping soul
of a heart that closed its door.
Some words need not be spoken
as silent eyes just say it all,
the language of two lovers who,
know all they can do, is fall.

KINDRED SPIRIT

        give to me
      the girl
    who'll chase the moon,
     who talks only of
    the moment,
    the girl who dances for
  the crashing waves
    with sand between her toes

and I'll pour
the whiskey,
   and make a promise
to stop the sun from rising

TROUBLED PASTS

She's got to where she's going,
through a journey that's unplanned
and she's made it through the worst of times,
with no one to hold her hand.
I listen to her stories, and,
every single word I feel
and the more I learn about her,
the more this fantasy is real.
She's kept it all inside so long,
but there between the lines
she's allowing me to read her,
and I recognise the signs.
The walls are coming down,
and she beckons me inside
to share every single smile she's had,
and every time she's cried.
There's more depth to her for sure,
than she'll care to show to all.
There's more strength inside than a lioness,
to overcome each fall.
I know now how she's fought,
to win the chance to claim this life
from the clutches of despair,
that cuts through hope like a knife.
I've never seen the weak of her,
yet she tells me that it's been
a visitor to her lonely nights,
and haunted her in dreams.
But she's never failed to triumph,
and she's never given in
and she's strived to create a world that's right,
for her children to live in.
Many things may not have happened,
because of choices made

but the light she shines from laughter,
has made her shadows fade.
I see more of her with all she shares,
and I'm connecting deeper every day
and she looks at me with passions eyes,
and takes my fears away.
Two troubled pasts have somehow,
found a way to both entwine
and I'm promising with every breath,
I'm going to make her future mine.

MOSAIC

Then you realise
that there wasn't a time
that they even loved you.
So you collect the mess
of the pieces that
they left behind,
because somebody out there
is waiting to see
the beautiful mosaic of you.

DON'T FORGET, NO REGRET

Don't forget to end that call with "I love you".
Don't forget to blow them kisses as they go.
Don't forget to hold their hand when together
and don't forget to always let them know.
Don't end a single day with uncertainty.
Don't sleep with unspoken words on your mind.
Don't leave any doubt in the thoughts of those you love
or wait to say things, for time you may not find.
Take every moment, and make it ever lasting.
Don't hesitate, there's no time for "not yet".
You can't turn back and change the time that's passed,
so fill each second with no room for regret.

RED FLAGS

I've made mistakes, it's true,
so I'm destined for distraction.
Enticed by every bright red flag
that I see as an attraction,
and the warning signs are there
in plain sight for all to see,
still I sail my vessel to the rocks
with a sense of urgency.
When you play with fire, you get burned.
I know this because I live it,
well baby you might sink my ship
but I will not go down with it.

STUPID LOVE

They say
love is blind
but it isn't.
Love sees all
love feels all
love knows all,
and love chooses to ignore
all of the ugly bits.
Love isn't blind,
love is stupid.

MARIONETTE 1

She pulled my strings
and made me dance,
to every tune
she had to sing.
Those lovers eyes
were filled with lies,
of fake futures
she could bring.
Behind the mask
she wore for me,
disguised
she hid away,
the truth that I
was nothing more,
than a puppet
in her play.
The shows now over
I'm packed away,
with all her
old playthings,
a discarded toy
of a broken boy,
that's still tied up
in her strings.

MARIONETTE 2

Oh marionette, you pulled those strings
and made your people dance,
to any tune that you wished to sing,
you left nothing down to chance.
To work all of the angles
to fabricate your lies,
to keep your puppets dancing
with hands over their eyes.
And your songs you'd sing to keep them
firmly on their toes,
in shadows you cast over them,
to ensure nobody knows.
And the strings have worn until
each one has slowly frayed,
and puppets fall without them
as each now feels betrayed.
But without your shadow, so it seems,
light is just now dawning
and the puppets find their own tune
as each one sings out in warning.
Yet there you sit, with empty hands
and think you still have hold,
of the world once at your fingertips,
as the truth of you unfolds.
You have no power now you see
to make each dancer turn,
and the light that takes your shadow
is the fire, while worlds burn.
And you should be shedding tears
and yet still you sing your songs,
thinking you've still strings to pull,
you will never right your wrongs.

MORE ALIVE

I never knew that I was shaded
until you stepped out of my sun,
and I was only pain free
once the hurting had begun.
I learned to be alone,
in all my "togethers" with you,
and I only found my focus
when I knew not what to do.
I didn't know that I was leaving
until I saw myself arrive,
and now the love is dead,
you know,
I'm feeling more alive.

RED WINE

I may not be my own friend
and I question all my choices,
while I'm drowning in red wine
just to silence all the voices.
And all I have are words
but I've used them all before,
now eloquence escapes my lips
they'll just drink what I will pour.
Your name will never leave my head
and the memory of you,
will forever make me smile
over all we ever knew.
And I can't say I've regrets
as I'd take back not one day,
reliving every moment
but let you heal in your own way.
Maybe somethings are just
never meant to last,
so I'll just love you from a distance
while I pour another glass.

MY EVERYTHING

Don't tell me not to get my hopes up,
don't tell me that I should not dream,
don't tell me all that I believe in
might not be everything it seems.
I'm going to dance to the music that we're making,
I'm going to wish that my tomorrow bears her name,
I hear her breathing as she's sleeping there beside me,
somehow reality and dreams are now the same.
She's a reason, she's a fantasy,
she's a whirlwind of desire,
she's a purpose to my being,
she brings the fuel that lights my fire.
She's been a little lost at times,
yet she's strong and leads the way,
she's weak behind the walls she keeps,
she's the words I couldn't say.
She's the melody of make believe,
she's the song I'll always sing,
she's the truth and she's the future,
she is just... my everything.

OVERTHINKING

I deliberate, I contemplate
I over think too much about,
the positives I'm living
until they turn again to doubt.
And I am my own worst enemy
when things begin to go my way,
and I recall, the feeling small,
when disillusion came to stay.
There's got to be a reason why
I just fail to sail on through,
because your actions speak much louder
than any words could ever do.
I show my vulnerability
and I take down again my wall,
but fuck, each time I do that
I can't help but feel I'll fall.

MY PERFECTION

I made a wish upon a star,
it's childish, this I'm knowing
but I was out of hope
I didn't know where I was going.
So I looked up to the heavens
and across the cloudless skies,
I prayed to Gods of each religion
as I slowly closed my eyes.
I imagined what perfection was
and I built the image in my mind
of everything I've needed
but never had the luck to find.
She had a heart of gold, so caring,
she'd give more than she would take,
she'd be honest and sincere
she'd have no time for fake.
She'd have the smile of a goddess,
eyes that only angels do,
she'd be loyal and so faithful
every word she'd say was true.
She'd take care of all she loves,
she'd nurture and she'd support,
she'd re-write every lesson
that before her I'd been taught.
She'd make me once again
believe that I could be worthwhile,
and she'd take away my tears
and leave me just to wear my smile.
She'd take the heart I give to her
and she'd hold it close and tight,
she'd never break it or let it go
even through the darkest night.
She'd have a beauty like no other
and she'd wow when she glides in,

like a wonder of the world,
the only sight my eyes take in.
She would be nothing short of wonderful
and she'd leave stardust in her wake,
I pictured all that she would be
in every wish that I would make.
Then I opened up my eyes again
and my dreams, they all came true,
as standing there before me
my perfection, girl, was you.

TREASURES

This world, may bring us
so many unexpected
twists and turns,
but it seems that
when you trip over stones in your path,
sometimes...
just sometimes,
you land right beside treasures
you'd never find
without
falling
first.

MAGICAL

The mountain will not crumble
nor the oceans, shall run dry,
the birds will not keep silent
or the blue, run from the sky.
The wind will blow, and ever more
the cloud will bring us rain,
the sun may seem to disappear
but at dawn, returns again.
The stars will not fail to shine
the fish, will never leave the sea,
as waves follow the majestic moon
while the shore waits patiently.
Some things just are, the way they are,
some things be, just what they be.
No miracle, though, as magical,
as the love you mean to me.

WHAT IF?

What if now is the time?
What if here is the place?
What if they are the one?
What if this is the pace?
What if the stars align?
What if the choice is made?
What if the futures bright?
What if what's behind you fades?
What if you've got it right?
What if there's no feeling wrong?
What if you can just make it happen?
What if weakness makes you strong?
What if there is no other way?
What if everything is cool?
What if you're finally on a winning streak?
What if you're no longer the fool?
What if you believe all that they say?
What if they prove in all they do?
What if you no longer have doubts?
What if....?
What if this could just be true?

THE FUTURE YET UNSEEN

I have wandered, lost and lonely,
felt alive in empty spaces,
held on too long, to icy hearts
and stared into vacant faces.
I've professed a love, to fakers
and been taken for a fool,
I've stayed longer than I should have
and disregarded my own rules.
I'd been taught that trust is worthless,
I've been shown that faith is cheap,
I've wasted way too many worries
on promises they don't keep.
My fractures, still have edges
that could cut the hands that bring repair,
at times the hope that fills my heart
is overshadowed by despair.
Yet I see the eyes that now see me
are filled with a futures dream
and finally I'm believing,
that some things, are as they seem.
My walls are down and once again
belief is in my mind,
that truth and love and honesty
are leaving all my doubts behind.
She is to me, the remedy
and her love becomes my cure,
and my scars are being healed as
the words she speaks are pure.
I'm destined to spend forever
on a journey led by fate,
and finally I've found the one
who's truly my soul mate.
So let's step into tomorrow
so far away from all that's been,

let's banish thoughts of doubtfulness
and claim this future, yet unseen.

CONTENTMENT

Occasionally,
you get to sit
alone
with nothing but your own thoughts
as company
and just relish
in the fact,
that
despite the arduous and treacherous
path you've walked,
you've reached a place
that is blissfully happy
and contented as fuck,
and I'm fortunate enough
to be able to say
I'm there.

TALKING IN TONGUES

There's electric once again
and sparks are truly flying,
as I taste your breath once more
take it away, as you are sighing.
My hands no longer empty
as they glide silently to find,
the journey of your contours
that I've travelled in my mind.
I know that as I'm touching,
the responses that I feel
are telling all the secrets,
your soul wants to reveal.
All your passion has been hidden
and I am feeding from your light,
to bring you to my darkness
and lose you in my night.
There's fire and there's truth
in the words you cannot speak,
as I talk to you in tongues
that makes your body weak.

NOT ALONE

At times the pain becomes unbearable
it feels so heavy from within,
as if I'm sinking deep inside the darkness
and there's no way I can win.
The challenge to pull myself back out
is beyond the strength that I possess,
the very weight of it becoming more
as I feel that I'm becoming less.
I feel these emotions,
and believed they were only mine,
but the more I learn that they are shared
helped my inner light to shine.
To know that there's so many
who have felt exactly what I feel,
who have risen back onto their feet
while life tried to force them just to kneel,
it gifts me hope and gifts me trust,
gifts me faith that I can fight
against the darkness that consumes me,
to fuel the fire of my light.
I am not alone it seems
and these feelings are not unique,
but each and every one of us
at times will still feel weak.
But knowing that we are all
swimming in the same deep oceans,
gives me the strength I need to balance
and to handle these emotions.

LEARNING TO BE ME

I'm no longer lost within myself,
my shedded skin behind
falls silently upon the past,
in the shadows of my mind.
Though the trials, bestowed upon me
and the winds that push me back,
cause fractures in the failings
of the fortune that I lack,
I rise and face the incoming
tides of tears, waves of regret,
that still wash over my sorry soul,
as solitude pays my debt.
I am no longer who I was
but not yet who I'll be,
in this limbo state of middle ground,
I'm learning to be me.

NOBODY AROUND

If you ask me, then I'll give to you,
if you speak, you know I'll hear.
If you want me to, I'll hold your hand
and I'll wipe away each tear.
I will comfort you, and be there,
my compassion drives each deed,
rely on me, turn to me,
I always have just what you need.
Be you lover, be you stranger,
be you family, be you friend,
you know I'll never walk away,
on me you can depend.
But in my sadness, when I turn
and each time I think I'll fall,
when the world is just too tough for me
and my back's against the wall,
as my eyes begin to fill
and my voice loses all its sound,
I find my hands are reaching out
to every nobody around.
There's no solace in my solitude,
my tears simply fall when I have cried
and each unspoken word, is only heard
by the no-one at my side.

AMONG THE ASHES

I live among the ashes
where fires used to burn,
and I warm myself on memories
of the love that won't return.
Thrown away the final piece
of my soul, to watch it fly,
past your tower that encased
a heart set to deny.
Did you ever feel me?
Did you ever walk in time?
To the musical words you spoke
when you said that you were mine.
I am feeling first the anger
from the lies within the talk,
as the music, it stopped playing
and I'm left alone to walk.
But then comes pain, and follows
is the emptiness that fills,
the chasm deep within my chest
from where the love for you still spills.
My sneering lip at the mirror
as the only hate I feel,
is for the wasted man that I've become
for thinking love was real.

PARADOXICAL

There's a haze of the unknown
beyond confusion, way past doubt,
of a misty eyed and melancholy
silent whispered shout.
Turning round to head back forwards
and taking time to rush on in,
to the start of what has ended
and finish what I begin.
While the remedy is what brings pain
and the killer is the cure,
of a mind that once lost heart,
that's in a head that's still unsure.
Always losing what has been won,
then I chase while run away,
from the darkness of the night-time
and hiding from light of day.
There's s presence felt by absence
of a solitary crowd,
and the thoughts I keep inside my lips
I am speaking them out loud.
There is no ink upon the page
and the story isn't yet complete,
but the tales that I'm telling,
seem to taste so bittersweet.
The only knowing that I'm feeling
is that my love was there to keep,
and yet it slipped through hands too full to hold
the emotions that run deep.
I'm a clueless paradoxical
contradiction of a man,
and to understand just what I need
I must understand just who I am.

THE THIEF OF SELF BELIEF

You will reach that point
where you can't see,
the difference between the demons
and the cavalry.
What's sent to save you, starts to scare you
and what slaughters, still alive,
thriving in that place
you need to let go to survive.
You still hold onto, what hurt you,
as the only real believing
is in the feeling of mistrust
and the faith in their deceiving.
Lovers eyes with no disguise
come to find you in your night,
but there's still solace in your shadows
and discomfort in their light.
So used to the abuse
of all the love so freely taken,
by the thief of self-belief
and each nightmare you were awake in,
and yes, your head is speaking
in a language that they've taught,
filled with a poison of persona
from the bitter words you bought.
Let them take you as they find you
yes, you're broken so don't try,
to make sense of the pretence
of each fake smile and hidden cry.
It's going to take sweet time
as you're learning to let go,
of the memory of misplaced trust
that haunts you with its echo.
So live and die in this life

with every chance you have to feel,
let the pain just refrain
long enough to see what's real,
and manifest itself in self health,
brought about, by headlong healing,
don't watch the graves of your tomorrow's
fill with the days that they're still stealing.

CHANGED

They change you,
when they break you.
They leave you different,
harder to love and with
less affection for others.
They change you in such a way
that nobody will ever get
the best version of you again.
That's the worst part I think,
You're left with less to give.

WHOLE

I was born with a mind filled with discontent,
I was raised in a way I wanted more.
I was gifted with a life that's never good enough,
my mirror, dissatisfied with what it saw.
There's been seasons that have kept all my summers cold,
there's been tidal waves of turmoil and of shame.
There's been days I've wished to end, when they've just begun,
and thoughts that drive me wild, I could not tame.
I've been left high up on a shelf, just to gather dust,
I've lived within the shadows I have cast.
I've prayed that when tomorrow comes it brings my dreams,
and I've woken up again still in my past.
There's a never-ending feeling of self-doubt I hold,
there's a knowing that I'm failing every test.
There's a weight I carry forward every day with me,
that I'm not good enough despite my very best.
I used to lose the battle daily just to keep afloat,
above the self-imposed fractures of my soul,
but then whispered softly came the words
"you are good enough"
And in the reflection of those eyes, I was whole.

DISDAIN

This life is not for me it seems
this body is a waste,
it clothes the bones that have no home
I could leave without a trace.
No other standing by me
to catch me when I fall,
no legacy of lovers
like I was never here at all.
There's no tears for my sorrow,
no hand to hold my own,
no ears to hear my stories
as I echo here alone.
Heavy chested palpitations
and an aftertaste of doubt,
sits upon my poisoned tongue
and cannot be spat out.
The midnight sky above me
hides the stars behind a cloud,
and I feel my insignificance
my tilted head now bowed.
I'd ask the heavens to take me
but I know that I must dwell,
in this lonely world I have created
that's so much worse for me than hell.

MY OWN DISEASE

Crashing waves wash over me in calm seas,
Feeling wrong when everything's so right.
Devil on my shoulder chases angels away,
and I still find the darkness in the light.
There's a wind that's blowing even when the clouds are still,
the rain will soak me through on driest summer days,
there's a tear that's hidden in the smiling eyes I show,
it seems I never really learn to change my ways.
I try with my best efforts, just to help them all,
and the only one is me I cannot please,
I carry weights upon my shoulders that I place there myself,
I'm everybody's cure, but I am my own disease.

DAMN YOU

Damn you for breaking me
and damn you for your lies.
Damn you for the stories told
while looking in my eyes.
Damn you for every day
and damn you for every night,
damn you for all you did so wrong
in proving each doubt right.
Damn you for taking from me,
damn you for never giving back,
damn you for dimming my inner shine
just to leave me in the black.
Damn you for the pretending
and damn you for not being true,
damn you for making me love again
just to then damn me, girl, damn you.

YOU JUST DON'T GET IT

I don't think you get what's going on right now,
you can't see the pain behind the smile.
I don't think you would even fit the shoes I wear,
you don't know the effort I put in to walk a mile.
You don't see the juggling of sanity,
and you can't feel the waves of despair,
you have no idea how hard it is to make it through a day
and if you did, would you even care.
I'm not blessed with a never-ending source of strength,
and anxiety is the companion of my sleep,
there are no tears to be seen in my smiling eyes,
but my chest holds a heart that will weep.
I'm a solitary figure even in a crowd,
I'm a man who knows to hide what I feel,
and just because I look like I'm flying through this life,
does not mean the weight that I carry isn't real.

BLISS

Bring to me the passion
and give to me the pure,
I'll return to you with real
and gift you with my raw.
My dreams I will deliver
to you with every kiss,
and in the warmth of your embrace
I will grant your every wish.
I'll meet your dark with sunrise
and for your empty I will give,
the hope your heart has longed for
with the reasons that I live.
Each secret of my soul
I'll tell to your listening ear,
and have faith that in my future,
you will always be right here.

HOMELESS HYMN

Concrete underfoot gives sound
to heavy feet upon this ground,
step through puddles, kick the stones
lonely heart and weary bones.
The hustle bustle behind the glass,
Danish pastry and latte glass,
caught sight of self in mirrored view
the window truths revealed to you.
Two sides of life come face to face
the coffee public, and street disgrace,
same world, same air, same blood, same chance,
envy and pity, in just one glance.
Curiouser and curiouser, what gives a man the right
to judge and form opinion, without knowing another's fight,
this is real and not no wonderland, and Alice is an ass
to tut and scoff, peer down her nose, through the looking glass.
Concrete underfoot, the tune
to a life that's over far too soon,
the street sign becomes his epitaph
as the cafe clique, just chat and laugh.
Ignorance is bliss they say
and so to look but never see,
is to let fragile lives just slip away
to the smell of ground coffee.

THE LAST LOST BOY

I want to tell a story
about a boy who was lost in time,
failed to fit in all the boxes
always asking "what is mine?".
A tortured heart torn inside out,
a mind not free for thinking,
forever was a sentence, locked,
in a ship destined for sinking.
I want to silence all the doubters
and open eyes of all the blind,
that he only needed seeing,
to not leave him behind.
Oh an anchored soul, will not be free
and to fly is fantasy,
all the love he held, he gave away
leaving none for him to see.
The world was never giving to
the boy lost in his head,
and the body may be living but,
the man inside was dead.
I want to tell a story,
of a man who learned to live.
One chance, to dance, to learn to love,
her heart would only give.
With open eyes, and no disguise
she gave to him his wish,
to just learn to be himself again,
she sealed his future with a kiss.

EMBERS TO ASHES

She is the one, she is the galaxy,
she is the very air I breathe.
She's the life force running through my veins
yet my eyes just watch her leave.
I once felt her hand in mine,
like it never would let go,
and in each resounding heartbeat
her name would just echo.
I used to hold her tightly
and now my hands can't even reach,
to touch her, and to tell her
I lack the skills of speech.
She is here, and at the same time gone,
I see only sadness in her stance,
and the music no longer plays for us
that used to lead us both to dance.
Inside I'm screaming please come back,
every emotion calls her name,
yet my lips are remaining sealed
as I know she no longer feels the same.
I have loved her, and I've lost her,
I have let gold slip through my fingers
and the words I cannot say out loud,
it's just a memory of love that lingers.
I miss her yet she's nowhere else,
but I've felt that she's not here,
I have to let her go her way
but can't watch her disappear.
I never gave enough of me
for her heart to realise,
that it was safe here deep within my own
and now I watch as her love dies.
Too much, too little, too slow, too late,
no fight left in me to take

back this girl whose fire died,
and left my heart to break.
There's no greater torture
in hell, or heaven above,
to stand and watch somebody
slowly falling out of love.

WALKING WITH THE STARS

I take a walk amid the stars at night
across the blanket of the sky,
I catch each one along the way
and whisper wishes through a sigh.
That the dreams I have while sleeping,
will come true when I awake,
that the love you have to give
is mine to always take.

FAR FROM PERFECT, FAR FROM PITIFUL

I was born on the wrong side of lucky
and I've wandered ever further from my fate,
I've lost my heart, too often to be proud of,
and even when I die, I'll turn up late.
I've helped out strangers, sometimes without knowing,
I've failed friendships that I thought would always last,
I've sailed my ship through stormy whiskey bottles,
yet I'll survive to always raise another glass.
A smile will greet me almost everywhere I go
and the band will always play for me, my tune,
every handshake meets me on arrival
but my feet are always leaving far too soon.
I've seen the eyes, that shy away when noticed
and I've seen behind the worn masks of fake pride,
I've wiped away the tears, when truth hurts,
and I've stood there and just nodded as they've lied.
I'm a nobody, a someone, and I'm all.
I am calm and chaos, clever, foolish, and I'm free.
I've hit rock bottom, while somehow standing tall,
far from perfect, far from pitiful, just me.

YOU JUST CAN'T KEEP ME DOWN

I'm not lost amongst the ruins
of a past built from decay,
been slowly moving forwards
when I couldn't see the way.
And I'm standing when it's time to fall,
smile when I should frown,
with the world upon my shoulders,
you just can't keep me down.
I've got blisters on my fingers,
my cheeks are tear stained,
every step I take is heavy,
my energy is drained.
I walk alone in solitude
like my life is a ghost town,
with the world upon my shoulders,
you just can't keep me down.
With all due respect
I expect no perfection,
with no regret,
served each debt, on collection.
Don't suggest it's a test
to find moral direction,
I'm a man with a plan,
this is my resurrection.
I pave the way to progress
through all of my mistakes,
I win more than I lose
no matter what life takes
My heads been under water
yet still I didn't drown,
with the world upon my shoulders,
you just can't keep me down.

DARK DILEMMA

Caught in a dark dilemma
of a thought I cannot think,
The raging tides inside my mind
so deep I know I'll sink.
Delusion of despair
and an inner demon taunts,
the ego into disbelief
from a past that ever haunts.
Never knowing where I'm going
and faith is fast at fading,
peering into my own eyes
from reflections I'm evading.
Sometimes a smile is just disguise,
sometimes a tear hides behind,
sometimes my hand is reaching outwards,
for another I can't find.
Rejection is my ally
and it devours self-esteem,
the voices of my nightmares
still silencing my dream.

NO PLACEBO

I count the complications carelessly,
I dismiss drama just to dance.
I feast on forever thoughts
of the golden glitter from your glance.
I had my demons for disciples
and I'd given up the ghost,
thinking love was just placebo
but now I've overdosed.
You are the bullet with my name on,
your heart is the loaded gun,
we said we'd just shoot for the moon
but now we're blowing up the sun.

THE KING OF CATASTROPHE

I am the king of catastrophe
the bumbling fool who breaks,
the fragile with his fingertips,
the master of mistakes.
I am the pilot of poor choices,
I drive myself into despair,
I hurt by having too much heart,
I create chaos, as I care.
And I don't mean to damage
all the treasures that I touch,
but some souls are suffocated
as once more I love too much.

DANCING FEET

Play to me your music
and I'll sing to you my song,
and though your heart won't know the words yet
soon it will sing along.
And as the notes across the air
flow to the rhythm of your beat,
my soul will take yours by the hand
and they'll find their dancing feet.

GROW YOUR ROSES

I know the rain is falling for you hard now
and I know the sun never seems to shine,
while you've lost a little of what used to be yourself
and you tell anyone that asks that you're just fine.
There's doubt that creeps on in to your day dreams
and there's ashes where your passions used to be,
the tunnel goes on endlessly with no light
and tomorrow is just too far for you to see.
Bad days just seem to outweigh all the good ones
and your greatest friend has now become despair,
you feel that you're alone, in mind, body and in soul
and your hands reach out, to nobody who's there.
I just want to tell you that you're not the only one,
I want to tell you that this will all become your past.
Look inside yourself, you'll find the strength to stand back up
and walk freely from the shadow that you've cast.
Salvation of the self comes from letting regret go,
the prize of pride is yours, when you can find inside,
that the roses will grow, from the earth below your feet,
because you've watered them with every tear you've cried.

THE ANGELS

I create my own disasters
then I lose the will to live,
with nothing left inside me
but the emptiness I'm with.
I cannot look into my own eyes
and I despise my every thought,
while digging deeper holes to delve in
I never learn from what I'm taught.
Pained by past decisions,
always wishing to rewind,
imagination fails to foresee futures
through my minds eye that is blind.
Cutting ties of craved connections,
I love enough to set them free.
Standing silently in solitude,
oh won't the angels come for me.

WALK AWAY

Sometimes we walk away to save others,
sometimes we walk , ourselves to save
Sometimes we walk away because we're weak,
sometimes we walk because we're brave.
There's times we walk to hurt
and times we walk to heal,
we walk away because we're numb inside
but then we walk because we feel.
We walk away because we're lost,
we walk in order to be found,
we walk away because of conflict
or we walk because of common ground.
There'll be a time to walk for silence
then we'll walk sometimes to talk,
we'll all get to where we're going to
because everyone will walk.

THE ANSWERS

I know that you always look for answers,
to all the questions, that you've never asked,
and you puzzle to figure out my inner thoughts,
wondering just what it is that lies behind the mask.
I know you want to know if secrets
live in the words that I have never said,
but there is only ever you, and you alone
that fill the thoughts that chase around my head.
I know you've been left confused by others,
about just what it was, that you could've done so wrong.
I know your doubts are made, from the tissue of your scars,
that were there before I ever came along.
Nobody ever had the right to hurt you
and I know you've learned that's just what people do,
but no one, on this earth, could love you deeper
than my heart, that simply beats for you.

SPACE TO GROW

There's a beauty that can follow
the breakage of a heart,
and though it feels like the end
it's just a place the "new" can start.
Just like the cracks in concrete
once the sunlight follows showers,
those places that are broken
become the home of growing flowers.
I know it hurts and yes, it's true,
those cracks may always show,
it's that place that pain exists right now
that new love has space to grow.

SOME DAYS

some days I feel like screaming
some days I want to hide
some days the world's my oyster
some days I feel denied
some days the sun is shining
some days I'm drowning in the rain
some days I'm lost inside myself
some days I'm found again
some days I'm trying to escape from me
some days I'm winning all I try
some days I have no questions
some days I'll just ask why?
some days I pray for nightfall
some days I fear the dark
some days I fail to shine
some days I am the spark
some days I am below my best
some days I am above
some days I'm empty and I just wish for
those some days that I feel loved

TIME TO HEAL

Cascaded torrent of crimson tide,
lashing through rivers of fake love applied,
the wrench of a grip that's too hard to breathe
or the weaknesses felt when too soft to believe.
Scorned lover, another, who lies to succeed
in puncturing hearts just to see if they bleed,
you're awaiting return of what's given, but fail
to get back what's invested, after acts of betrayal,
to willingly break and to watch a soul fall,
belittling an ego, and then making it crawl.
Only one option, to sever the ties
of toxic delusion and devils' disguise.
The secret of sanity is now to talk,
don't lock up emotion, don't run, but first walk,
there's rebuilding in progress, there's time to be taken
for a neglected heart that has slept, to awaken.
Be careful your damage may just be too much
and cause nothing but pain to the next one to touch.

CURSED

I am just a vessel, who is lost inside the rain,
been more than once to hell, and I am headed there again
and I am just a bit part, in the stories that I write,
a paper town upon a map, that's lost and out of sight.
And I'm just trying to be better
and somehow I end up worse,
watching dreams through whitewashed windows
as I can't escape the curse.
There's a deafening white noise, and the smell of stale perfume,
the liquors hitting harder in a nicotine-stained room,
melodies bring memories, a melancholy feel,
lyrics written in scar tissue, that time itself can't heal.
And I'm just trying to be better
and somehow I end up worse,
watching dreams through whitewashed windows
as I can't escape the curse.

I've prayed in the churches, of Gods from each religion
but it seems there isn't one that has belief in me,
I've paid all my dues, once, twice, a million times,
still the devil came and took my soul for free.

BACK DOWN THE RABBIT HOLE

The barricade that I create
becomes my prison wall,
isolation for self preservation
weak from the baggage that I haul.
Anxiety, I try to be,
bigger than my blues.
Head buried in the avalanche
of the sanity I lose.
Always prone to stand alone,
solitude's a friend to me.
Locked behind the reasons why,
loneliness my enemy.
Detect my own reflection
looks upon me with disdain,
a counterpart to each false start,
I hit the ground again.
Rationality walks out on me,
predict my own demise.
Devastated by ill-fated thoughts,
a mood that darkens stormy skies.
Each sight of something brighter
sets up, to fail, my sorry soul,
and gives reasons to my demons
to push me back down the rabbit hole.

WALK OF SHAME

Walking in the early hours
to soothe my sorry soul,
the stars show to me, misfortune
of the path ahead she stole.
The waves my only melody
that keep my thoughts in tune,
to finding new ways forward
and rediscover myself soon.
A lifetime in a moment
and a moment that shall last,
forever, and yet never,
a future wish lost in the past.
Oh moonlight won't you guide me
to where the sun, again shall rise,
and rain, please wash away the pain
that has been leaking from my eyes.

THE TRUTH

The truth lives there, in that moment, when you
close your eyes and allow your breath to be stolen.
When words flutter away like butterflies, when
reason blooms like flowers in the sun, and when
doubt is kept at bay like the dew drops on a web at
dawn.
The truth does not speak and does not
protest, nor does it explain itself.
Truth lives there, in that moment that love
is first felt between two lost souls
who find themselves together.
Nothing matters but that kind of love,
and that, right there,
is truth.

UNSCRIBBLED

Empty notebooks
and a guitar that never plays.
There's no words and there's no music,
just a mind lost in the haze.
The clocks are spinning forwards
and the days just seem to melt,
into memories of feelings
that soon I forget I've even felt.
Dust on my piano
and a pen filled with dried ink,
no poetic justice
when there's no time left to think.
A full head of empty thoughts
and not a single word to share,
lips that can no longer speak
above the silence of the air.
Empty pages of emotion
in the blank void that is my curse,
Emotive eulogy is shown now
in my unscribbled sentimental verse.

THE PRECIPICE

Oh what have I become,
all wrong choices steered the course,
to a life of self abandonment,
regret, the driving force.
Tired eyes return my glances
and I feel inside I'm knowing,
that outwardly this cannot be seen
my self-loathing never showing.
I'm standing on the precipice
of every broken pledge,
and knowing moving forwards
takes me closer to the edge.
Life is hanging in the balance
of the threads I failed to weave,
and the discontent in my reflection
Is all that I believe.
Too many times I've lived to hate myself,
too often I have disdain
for the fact I've lived another day
to simply just remain.
Ever failing ever falling,
ever disappointing to all those
who gave me second chances,
yet let them down again, I chose.
I'm a nothing and a nobody,
I'm a never was or will be,
I'm the lost and I'm the lonely,
I am the very worst of me.
The end I know is nearing
as I despise all that I am,
and I look in hope that I'll be saved
by you, the mirror man.

SMITTEN

They speak of hearts and souls
and relationship goals,
holding hands and sunset walking.
Star filled skies,
looking into her eyes,
sweet nothings, pillow talking.
Sunrise, sunset
not one regret,
each day, as yet, unwritten,
Futures unfold,
three words are told
and she, it seems, is smitten.

SEAGLASS

I am sea glass
once fragile
once sharp,
but torrents
have shaped me
and now
you can fumble
my edges
through your
fingers
without cutting,
and still see, that
despite the
raging tides that
I have been
subject to,
my colours remain
unchanged.

THE EXCEPTION TO THE RULE

you could be the reason, the exception to the rule,
every lesson that I've learned, that they didn't teach at school.
or you could be the smoke, that is clouding my view,
but I will always be the one, who makes their way to you.
you could be the coffee, that is filling up my cup,
that sweet kick of caffeine, that I needed to get up.
or you could be the whiskey, that is chasing every beer,
but I will always be the one, that waits for you right here.
you could be the anti-venom, that saves my poisoned blood,
the aftermath of chaos, that always follows flood.
or you could even be the devil, you can never really tell,
but I will always be the one, who follows you to hell.
you may just be so wrong for me
you may just be so right
you may just let me fall, but then
you may just fuel my flight
you may just show all that you are
you may just keep it hidden
you may just be the one for me, or
you may just be forbidden
you could be the truth, between every spoken lie,
the wind that breaks the clouds, to let sunshine through the sky.
you could be the answer, or you could be a warning sign,
but I will always be the one, who just tries to make you mine.

LOVE YOURSELF MORE

You can't build your bridges from apologies.
You can't sail your ship of sorry through the tide.
You can't fly through the skies, that are clouded with regret,
you've got to just forgive yourself and let it slide.
Taking self-loathing for your company,
and bringing all your hatred for the ride,
will stop you in your tracks, like stones inside your shoes,
and to move on, there's only you who can decide.
Take time to repair, and to adjust your point of view.
Try to see the beauty of within.
So you made a few mistakes but so did everyone,
there are only angels up above us, without sin.
There's no room on your path for discontent.
There's no passage through the rough, found easily.
There's still mountains to climb, from the molehills you ignored,
but you've got to learn to love yourself to set you free

THE BIG BAD WOLF

Sometimes I talk to the world,
while I hide myself away
with all the thoughts inside my head,
that I just can't bring myself to say.
Seeking kindness from the friends
to who I refuse to just reveal,
every doubt and insecurity
instead I'm choosing to conceal.
Behind my smiling eyes I hide,
wearing a mask of my faked laughter,
I paint a picture of a fairy tale
and act like it's "happy ever after".
In truth the big bad wolf is coming
and my mind's a house of straw,
with every self neglecting imposed thought
he's blowing at my door.
I look towards those closest
for the help I'm needing for this task,
to openly bare my wounds of doubt
yet I can't face them honestly to ask,
how to build my inner house of bricks,
how to secure myself inside.
How to believe in all the good of me
and make each bad thought of me subside.
He's huffing and he's puffing still,
self-worth, like straw, flies round
and I'll sit alone amongst the debris,
as my house falls to the ground.

WHO AM I?

Who am I, if not me?
When I fail to feel myself.
I won't let another fall behind,
but I always leave me, on the shelf.
I gave a lifetime to pleasing everyone
and never quite got figured out,
how to make myself smile, by being me,
Instead I've been courted by self-doubt.
You'll never see a person in my company,
who doesn't feel like they're the one,
because I give and I care, and I elevate
each other person to make them strong.
But the weak of me I keep at bay
from any eyes that may just pry,
and my laughter shows them a happiness
that always hides the fact I cry.
I'm a little lost but won't admit it,
I'm downbeat but they won't see,
because I masquerade as the life and soul
to hide away the real me.
It's not to fool or give pretence,
it's not to deceive, not to be fake,
but my smile is so damn fragile,
that if I didn't share it, I would break.

TAKE MY HAND

If somebody had told me
that you would walk on in,
to the emptiest of rooms
that I always found myself in.
I wouldn't listen, wouldn't hear a word,
I really wouldn't say
a single thing that might just,
give my heart away.
Unfolding maps of where I've walked along,
so long now all alone,
tracing tracks of tear-stained journeys,
just to find my own way home.
And if somebody had told me
that you would stay a while,
to take my hand and join my fallen place,
and to give to me, my smile.
I wouldn't look, wouldn't see it coming,
I wouldn't know
a single thing about the unexpected
feelings that would grow.
Deciphering the stars above
and trying to decide,
if fate is sending messages
or if the angels lied.
And if somebody had told me
that you'd be my saving grace,
from the moment that you said hello
and first I saw your face.
I would not believe in this impossible,
would not trust that you could be
the one to unchain my heart,
and who could for once just set it free.

NECTAR

Astounding
the strength we
hold on to
misery
and the ease
at which we
lose grasp of happiness.
Like the chinks
of swirling
ice cubes,
rolling around
the bottom of
an empty
whiskey glass,
wondering
where all
the nectar
has gone.

THE PAIN THAT BINDS US

The seconds on the clock, tick slowly,
the days, they pass, too fast.
We cling on, to all, we used to feel,
to make the memories last.
The heart it breaks, and breaks again,
this is the story, that we tell,
and our tears, fall over lifetimes,
in which we lock ourselves in hell.
There's hope that's lost, and there's denial,
There is faith, sold down the river.
There's the warmth of love, that's left us,
with the cold of, a winters shiver.
We look around, and see the world,
through glazed eyes, that can't stop crying,
and right there, in that moment,
you realise, that you've stopped trying.
Alone in all the hurt, and then,
every ounce of you, chastises,
that there's nothing left, but the grief of love,
yet your head, just realises,
that every smile was built, from a place of hurt,
that each laugh, has followed tears.
Because each and every soul, on earth,
throughout their living years,
has those times they wish, to end it all,
has those times, that in despair,
they feel, that they're insignificant,
and that no other, would ever care.
But we sail through, the best of times,
and we ride the stormy weather,
in the knowledge that, we're not alone,
and it's the pain that binds us, all together.

Madness and Therapy

For all of those who ask "What does Mesentire mean?"

Here is your answer

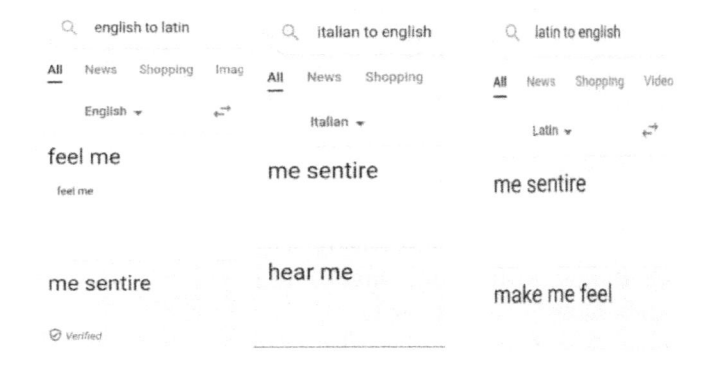

english to latin	italian to english	latin to english
English	Italian	Latin
feel me	me sentire	me sentire
feel me		
me sentire	hear me	make me feel
Verified		

Take your pick, though I like to think that it means all 3, feel me, hear me, make me feel.

Mesentire

Printed in Great Britain
by Amazon